BATTLE EARTH

NICK S. THOMAS

BATTLE EARTH

NICK S. THOMAS

CHAPTER ONE

21st March 2234.

Larson stepped across the barren surface of Mars in his self-contained suit. He carried a box full of samples that he'd collected that day. Approaching their shuttle he could see Ruby climbing aboard. It was a small ship, only ten metres long and able to carry just six passengers and limited cargo.

Mars was a research base. Humanity had reached the stars, but had done little to expand beyond the well-established Moon colony. Travelling times continued to prohibit further space colonisation, it taking twenty weeks to travel between Mars and Earth during the optimum time of alignment. Ninety-four people were stationed on the Mars research colony. For many years they had continued to develop the technology to develop the planet for further human usage. Ruby turned to see Larson moving towards their ship, she called to him through their intercom.

"All done?"

"Yeah, it never gets old does it?" asked Larson.

"Trust me, you spend a full year here, you'll soon grow tired of it."

Water had been discovered below the surface of Mars long ago, but the excitement of its discovery had soon died down. The research colony had existed for forty years. Terraforming was considered a vital research pursuit for those stationed there. While significant progress had been made in understanding how such a practice could be done, no developments had been made in implementing them.

With the established Moon colony, as well as the two successful space stations at LaGrange points L4 and L5, there had been little interest in budgeting immense amounts of government funds into developing a colony that would take several months to travel between. People accepted that Mars colonisation was an inevitable step for humanity. They just hadn't quite reached its necessity nor found a way of making it practical.

Larson stepped up to the boarding ramp of the shuttle and turned back to look at the planet's surface. It was a hard-edged and mountainous terrain that looked inhospitable to humans, but he still found it awe-inspiring. He only wished it was possible to walk on it without the cumbrance of his suit.

"Come on, it's almost lunchtime!" Ruby shouted.

Taking one last glance, Larson turned and carried on up the ramp and into the shuttle, placing his box onto the racks before the seating. The ramp sealed behind them and Larson tapped a small button on the collar of his suit. The clear dome-shaped helmet hinged back and vanished into the bulky shoulder section. He breathed in deeply. The shuttle's air source was far from the fresh air he loved so much on earth, but it was a relief after an hour inside the confine of his helmet.

"You know, Ruby, for someone who volunteered for this work you sure don't seem to care much for the planet."

"I care about it, and I'll be glad once we have got it terraformed. Until that time it's an ugly and lifeless wasteland."

"Just think about it, Earth was developed over thousands of years, I wonder how we would do if we could start entirely from scratch on a similar world."

"Don't expect any kind of paradise. Whenever we finally get this world going it will probably just look the same as anywhere else," Ruby replied.

"Such cynicism, alright, let's get back and you can enjoy your precious meal."

* * *

"This is Shuttle 12 to Ares, requesting permission to land, over."

"This is Ares, we have lost contact with Shuttle 5, you are requested to investigate at their last known co-ordinates which are being sent to you now, over."

"Confirmed, over and out," said Ruby.

"So much for your lunch break!"

She looked at her colleague with an annoyed grin. It was a lonely life on the Ares colony, with few luxuries in life. She turned back to the controls and re-directed to the co-ordinates they'd been given, three hours to the south of the camp.

"What do you think happened to them?" asked Larson.

"Probably just a communications fault, it happens from time to time."

* * *

Flying low over the canyon ridges the shuttle eventually approached the co-ordinates. The two researchers had left the colony ten hours previously and were feeling the fatigue kicking in. Unsure what they expected to find, curiosity kept them awake. As their ship soared over a large peak, the shuttle they were searching for came into view in the valley ahead.

"Exactly where they were supposed to be, so what's the problem?"

"We still need to check it out, Larson, they've been out of contact for hours."

She manoeuvred the shuttle down to a smooth landing just twenty metres from the other ship. Their shuttles ran an almost silent operation, with their highly advanced and efficient ion engines. They both flicked the switches to activate and enclose their suits and continue their personal oxygen supply.

"Grab one of the scanners, we'll see if you can track them down."

Larson sighed as he picked up the cumbersome device and slung it onto his back. The door lifted and the ramp lowered. They were once again stepping out onto the surface of the red planet. Larson looked again in awe at the harsh but fascinating and striking terrain.

"No sign of them, I'll try the shuttle," said Ruby.

Larson nodded, he was too busy taking in the view to care. Living in the knowledge that they were the only living inhabitants on the planet, they wandered freely about the surface with no worries. With the technology that they had at their fingertips, the limit of their oxygen supply was the only concern in their lives.

Ruby pressed the entry pad to the shuttle they had been sent to investigate. The door lifted and the ramp slid open, but no one was inside. She entered the vehicle looking around for any signs of their colleagues. Some of the research equipment was out.

"They can't be far," she said.

"Then why didn't they get in contact? They're just

wasting our time."

"Maybe they found something interesting and have been busy?"

They turned and looked around the valley. It was a familiar sight. Barren, with sharp mountain peaks and hard-edged rock formations. There was rarely anything to cause surprise on Mars. Everywhere but their research base was a lifeless and desolate plain.

"Alright, get the scanner out, Larson, let's see if we can find them."

He hauled the big case from his shoulders and placed it down on the hard rocky ground. He lifted the lid of the ruggedized computer. The oversized keys to allow operation in thick gloves made it appear as a caricature of their own personal devices. He tapped a few buttons and brought up a circular scanning device. It read movement within a hundred-metre radius. The dial began to spin and search for any signs of life.

As Larson watched the display, Ruby looked around the area of the ship. It was hard to find signs of footprints on the surface of Mars, it being so hard to rarely leave imprints. The dust often covered over what few signs of life were left.

"Got anything?" she asked.

"No, hang on, just got a reading!"

Ruby moved up to his side looking down at the screen as the dial continued to track around the scanner. She saw it flash once again as it got a reading. She squinted to look down at what it was.

"Four objects? I thought this was a standard two-man research team?"

"That's what we were told, maybe the scanner is reading wrong," Larson answered.

"Yeah, maybe. Let's go take a look, it's just over that ridge, you can leave that here."

Larson gladly shut the screen and stood up to follow her across the surface. Up ahead was a rock outcrop leading to another valley in the rocky terrain. They went along the surface, each anxiously wanting to know the explanation for the reading they had gotten. There was still plenty to learn from the planet of Mars, meaning the potential for exciting new developments was always on the cards.

They reached the outcrop and navigated their way through the obstacles. They always had to be careful of the sharp and jagged terrain of Mars, as damages to their mechanical counter pressure suits was far from ideal. The risk of radiation was a small concern in low dosages, the complex repair work afterwards plus the difficulty and expense of sourcing new equipment was more of an issue.

As Larson navigated the close terrain he noticed that Ruby had stopped up ahead, standing like a statue as she looked ahead. He moved to her side and stood with the same dumbfounded expression as she had on her face. In front of them was what appeared to be a ship of some kind, but its surface was almost identical to the Martian terrain, making it blend in like a chameleon.

The ship was twice the size of their shuttle and completely unrecognisable to them. It had a bulbous body and large engines, with wings protruding from its hull. The camouflage effect of its bodywork made it difficult to make out much more than a rough shape. Before they could study it any longer, their eyes were drawn to movement on the surface in front of the vessel.

They could see what appeared to be their two colleagues, wearing the same suits as them. One was kneeling down on the ground, the other stood beside him. Ten metres in front were two other figures, though substantially taller and not recognisable at all.

"Who the hell are they?" asked Larson.

Ruby pulled out her binoculars from a pouch on her belt. Tapping a small switch, they expanded out into a high power device. She lifted them and looked on in horror at what she saw.

"What is it?"

She was still speechless. Having run out of patience, Larson snatched the binoculars from her hands. She put up no fight and was still stunned, looking in on the scene in terror. Larson lifted the binoculars to see what had shaken her so badly. He couldn't believe what he was seeing. The two figures stood before their colleagues were well over two metres tall and wore some type of metallic armour.

Their suits appeared to have sprung lower leg mechanisms that more resembled a cat or dog standing on its back legs than a human. Their bodies tapered out into a broad chest section. A helmet-like device was embedded in the front of the suit, as if either they had no neck, or the suits were completely encapsulating their bodies. Larson was as fascinated as he was terrified by the sight. Nothing they saw resembled anything they had ever seen. A hundred questions began to roll around in his head, but before he could say another word, he saw the two figures lift something from their sides. Light flashed from the devices and their two colleagues spasmed with the impact of some kind of energy.

Ruby had to stop herself from screaming, realising that doing so would risk their lives. She dropped within the rock outcrop with Larson as they hid from sight.

"What the hell are they?" he asked her.

"I have no fucking idea!"

"Did they just execute those two people?"

"What do you think?"

"What the hell are we going to do?"

"I don't know, okay!"

Larson crept up from behind the rock face and peered out into the valley. The two figures strode towards their ship and into a small lifting device that hoisted them into the vessel. He looked down at the bodies, still lifeless on the hard ground. A low pulsing sound resonated from the peculiar ship as it began to lift off from the surface. Keeping low to the ground, it soared off in the opposite direction from where they had left their shuttle.

"Are they gone?" asked Ruby.

"Yes, what are we going to do?"

"Get the hell out of here!"

"What about them?" he pointed to the bodies of their fallen comrades.

"They're dead. I have no idea what we have just witnessed, but unless you want to follow them I suggest we make a run for it."

"Right, let's move!"

They got up from behind the rocks and made a dash for their ship, as quickly they could in the gravity on Mars. It felt like a long run back to the vessel. Despite the valley being just as tranquil and desolate as it previously was, they expected to be struck down at any moment. Larson arrived first, surprised to have made it. With seconds of getting aboard they were in the air. He reached for the intercom button to contact their colony.

"Wait!" shouted Ruby.

"What? We have to call this in!"

"And say what, that we just saw some unidentified beings kill two of our research team, but that we don't have any idea who or what they are, where they came from, or have any evidence to backup our story?"

"That doesn't change the fact that it happened," said

Larson.

"No, but this has to be handled properly. We need the base staff to take this seriously, not to think we have lost our minds."

"Alright, you do it."

She reached forward and hit the intercom switch. "This is Shuttle 12 to Ares, please come in, over."

"This is Ares Command, over."

"We have a Code Red, I repeat, Code Red, over."

There was an uncomfortable silence as they soared across the surface of the planet. Clearly their signal had caused a shockwave to the colony. Code Red was an emergency signal for extreme situations only, none of which they had ever experienced. Finally a signal came back over the radio.

"This is Morris, what the hell is going on?"

Morris was the research base commander, a leading scientist and project leader for over twenty years.

"Please switch to a direct and private channel, over," replied Ruby.

A few moments later the Commander came back on the line.

"You're on with me directly, explain to me what the hell is going on!"

"Sir, we just witnessed the execution of the crew of Shuttle 5 by two unidentified personnel, over."

"What? Where are they now?"

"They left heading south in a vessel which appeared to mimic the ground's surface and was approximately twice the size of our shuttle, over."

"Did you collect any data from the scene?"

"No, Sir, we left in fear of our lives. I advise an immediate issue of the Lee Protocol, over."

"Listen to me, Ruby, these are some extreme suggestions you are making, based on no evidence that you can present to me. I can't risk widespread panic based on hearsay."

"This is not a joke, Sir. We came close to death and some of our people were not so lucky. Now issue the damn protocol and lock the colony down!"

"I'll issue it, but you'd better be right about this or you'll be out the door!"

"Sir, I wish I wasn't, we'll be with you in just under three hours, be ready, over and out."

She turned off the intercom and continued to stare out at the ground as their shuttle darted across the rough landscape, hugging the terrain. Larson looked over to her, but it seemed she didn't intend giving anything up.

"Lee Protocol?" he asked.

"It's an emergency protocol calling for all weapons trained personnel to immediately arm themselves and prepare for imminent attack."

"We have a plan for that?"

"It was always a possibility, we just never expected it to actually happen."

"What did happen?" asked Larson.

"I really don't know!"

* * *

They finally caught sight of the Ares research colony, knowing they were all in big trouble. But somehow facing it in larger numbers made them feel much safer. The compound was still, all vehicle movement had been stopped and all exits sealed except for their docking bay.

"This is Shuttle 12 to Ares, requesting permission to land, over," said Ruby.

"Permission authorised, over."

The large steel doors slid open, revealing an almost full docking bay. Only their bay, Shuttle 5's pad and the freight loader area were empty. The doors quickly shut behind them, sealing the environment and allowing people to again walk freely. Ruby brought the shuttle down to a quick and smooth landing. They could see that Morris and several others of the senior research team were waiting for them. They all wore pressure suits and several had pistols slung on their waists. Ruby and Larson stepped out to greet their colleagues who were grim faced.

"You'd better start talking, Ruby," said Morris.

"I don't know how else to say this, Sir. When we arrived at the co-ordinates we found Shuttle 5 empty. We followed our scanner to the site of four readings, where we witnessed the execution of the shuttle's crew by two beings, the likes of which I have never seen."

"You saw this too?" asked Morris.

"Yes, Sir, they had a ship with some type of chameleon skin to it. Their weapons appeared to be energy based devices."

"Do we have any reason to think that any other organisations could be on the planet with us, Sir?" asked Ruby.

"Like who?"

"I don't know, a private company, or a foreign military."

"This is a joint operation by twenty-one countries, who would try and undermine that?"

Morris' intercom on his wrist crackled as a transmission came through from their command centre.

"Sir, we have three vessels incoming, they are not responding to..."

Before the operator could finish a huge explosion erupted in the entry doors to the docking yard. They were knocked off their feet by the blast.

"Masks on! Masks on!" Morris shouted.

Larson and Ruby hit the controls on their suits and slid their dome-topped helmets over to revert to their own oxygen supply. They huddled behind a stack of large crates and watched as three small vessels passed through the breach swooping in quickly to land in the wide-open area used for supply deliveries. The vessels were mimicking their surroundings just as the one did before, now replicating the grey metallic surfaces of the docking area.

Within seconds of landing, six figures emerged from them and were already shooting at any people they could see. Morris looked in horror as he drew his pistol.

"What do we do, Sir?" shouted Larson.

He didn't respond, only watched as four of their armed personnel tried to engage their armoured foes. The energy weapons fizzled as blue pulses ripped through the interior of the walls. Within seconds the defenders were lying dead on the floor of the docking bay, their bodies smouldering. Morris had quickly come to the same conclusion that they had previously. These were not humans.

The figures walked on thin metallic legs that appeared to be sprung, supporting their substantial bodies. They could only imagine that it was an armoured suit encasing whatever was controlling it. Morris turned back to Larson and Ruby.

"We are finished here, take your shuttle, you'll have enough power and supplies to reach the Moon colony. Get a transmission out immediately reporting what you have seen, they must be warned!"

"How are we going to get past them?" asked Ruby.

They turned back to watch as the six soldiers continued on into the heart of the colony. They were certainly on a mission to purge it. Morris looked back at the two men he had with him, each was armed with the same personal defence weapon he had in his hand.

"We'll try and hold them here as long as we can, you just get out and send that signal immediately!"

"What do they want from us?" she asked.

The shock had begun to pass as fear set in. All around them had long faces, they were realising that their lives were likely coming to an abrupt end. A number of the personnel had firearms training on the research colony, but never expected a need to use them.

"You know as much as I do, now get out of here!" shouted Morris.

He moved out from beyond the crates with the other crew and rushed to the door where the soldiers had gone through. They knew they were heading for their own deaths, but there was no choice left. Ruby and Larson watched as they reached the doorway. Morris looked back at them and nodded. They took the signal for what it was and leapt out from the cover and ran to their shuttle. The engines were fired up before the shuttle ramp was closed. Larson stumbled as they lifted off the docking bay floor as he was trying to make his way towards the cockpit.

"Come on, strap yourself in!" she shouted at him.

He jumped into the seat as she manoeuvred them out. He stared at the obscure ships occupying their docking bay. They were the same vessel type they had witnessed earlier. The ever-changing surface texture that camouflaged them against any terrain still made it difficult to fully make out any details on them.

"Time to get the hell out of here!"

She hit the power and they surged towards the smashed doorway where the attackers had blasted through. In seconds they burst out of the docking bay and quickly gained altitude. They had expected to see some monstrous vessel blocking their path, but there was nothing. Only the same barren and desolate landscape and sky they had become so accustomed. The shuttle broke out of the Mars atmosphere and into the cold darkness of space. There were still no signs of any other ships in the vicinity.

"We made it!" shouted Larson.

"Maybe."

Ruby reached forward and programmed the transmitter to send a direct and live feed to their sister organisation on the Moon colony.

"You're going to send it out live?"

"Yes, we have no idea how much time we have."

She took a deep breath and started the transmission.

"This is Shuttle 12 of the Ares research base. The colony has just been attacked by unidentified hostiles. We are the only known survivors. The attackers utilised a chameleon type technology on their ships and attacked without provocation or any form of communication. They were well equipped and ruthless."

"What's that on the scanner?" asked Larson.

She looked down to see an object approaching them from the planet at high speed.

"Hold on!"

The shuttle surged forward as Ruby put full power to their engines.

"At this speed we won't have enough power to reach any of the colonies!" shouted Larson.

"If we can't outrun these bastards it won't matter anyway!"

"They're still gaining on us!"

"Larson, are we still transmitting?"

"Yes!"

"This is Shuttle 12, we are under attack by what can only be described as alien forces, we cannot outrun them, do not..."

The shuttle was hit by a high power weapon that ripped it open killing both aboard instantly, the remnants floated apart in a fizzling array of twisted metal.

CHAPTER TWO

"Thirty seconds!" shouted Rains into the intercom.

The Eagle FV assault copter soared across the treetops like a vulture to its prey. 5.45am and the sun was just rising from the trees in the distance. Rains rubbed his eyes, feeling the early start more than usual. As a navy pilot he was conditioned to early morning operations but since their new joint operations, the Commander was pushing them hard.

Behind the cockpit of the copter sat ten U.S. marines. They each wore the Universal Camouflage Pattern (UCP), which was worn by all U.S., European Union and Alliance of Asia forces, as well as a number of smaller members of the UEN, United Earth Nations. After World War 3 there had been a more determined attempt than ever to unify the major powers in the world. The world had not seen a war between major powers for sixty years.

"Another fine day in the Marine Corps," said Captain Friday.

Mitch Taylor grinned at his second in command as he looked back out of the porthole. He could see the almost silhouettes of their other aircraft soaring along beside them, nine in his view alone. The Major led back in his seat and looked around at his HQ Squad to be sure they were ready. The side doors slid open.

"Let's do this!" shouted Mitch.

The copter's tail slung down as the vehicle came to an abrupt hover, the signal light turning green. Without wasting another moment the Major leapt from the door. It was a thirty-metre fall to the street below, close to the limits of their free fall boosters. They fired up within seconds of him feeling the open air, the auto-sensors doing their work.

Seconds later the ten marines hit the ground, their boosters ticking from the immense heat burn. They made a quick dash to the nearest building, not stopping to survey the terrain. They were more than familiar with their surroundings from endlessly studying the maps and intel of the area. Taylor knew it was only a training mission, but to treat it as anything but real combat could be detrimental to his soldiers in the future.

Suarez hit the wall beside him, peering around the corner into the street. The buildings were derelict but still perfectly serviceable for their purposes, one of the many reminders of what a world war could do.

"Where are the limey bastards?" asked Lieutenant Suarez.

Sergeant Silva knelt out in front of them behind a large piece of fallen concrete from a building that previously stood in their position. It was a hell of a temperature for a combat exercise. Each marine wore a minimum of sixty kilograms of gear. Body armour technology had got progressively better and lighter, but that just meant they wore more of it. The Falcon armour system gave coverage to most of their armour, except for inner joints and a few gaps.

"Guess it's too much to hope for that they didn't show up?" asked Silva.

"You can rely on the British bastards to be there, and they'll give you a good kick in the nuts if they catch you napping," said Taylor.

The Major looked around quickly surveying the situation, the one hundred and eighty strong marine unit had landed on target and in good time. It was a good start to what was becoming a gruelling day. It felt like they'd stepped out into the desert, of which the abandoned city of Reno was quickly becoming.

"Alright, let's move up," he ordered.

The throat mics added little weight to their payload but allowed them to stay in contact for up to thirty kilometres in open terrain. Looking around the empty streets there was little left to show that this had been a gambling hotspot of the state. Years of abandonment, followed by regular military training activities, had robbed it of any splendour. All that was left were the empty hulks of hotels, casinos and clubs, dust and sand filled.

They moved along quickly but cautiously through the eerily quiet streets, there were still the remnants of abandoned cars. Taylor looked around to see his teams pouring through the old city. They moved on three parallel streets, giving as much of a spread as they could manage. Up ahead he could make out the familiar shape of the former Cortez Casino which was their target.

The Major knelt down beside a rusted old car shell, it was so old that he couldn't even begin to identify its model, beyond the barely visible Cadillac symbol on the trunk. He pulled out his Infopad from his webbing and flipped it open. It had an edge-to-edge display and touch screen control. The map of their location displayed from when he'd last looked at it. Suarez huddled down beside him, his body armour slamming harshly into the rusted frame of the car.

"What is it?" he asked.

"I don't like it, a hundred metres from the target and no sign of resistance or even lookouts, Sir."

"Maybe they're waiting inside as they're supposed to?"

"Not a chance, Sir, they won't give it to us easy."

"Alpha and Delta swing wide, Bravo and Charlie down

the centre with me!" Taylor ordered.

Taylor could just see a glimmer of movement out of the corner of his eye as his teams moved forward in the adjoining streets. Their task was simple, to take the casino building, secure two VIPs and neutralise any hostiles. However the reality was that they were facing a British parachute regiment platoon from the European Union Army (EUA). Despite having numerical superiority, they were going in blind.

"Move up!"

He got to his feet and continued forward at an almost jogging pace keeping his upper body hunched low. One of his men spasmed, he dropped to the floor unable to move.

"Contact!" shouted Taylor.

He looked over at his downed comrade. The devices they wore on their armour during training sent a small pulse through their gear when hit by simulated fire, it momentarily incapacitated the target. The weapons they used were running blanks with the training device fitted, meaning they could simulate both the atmosphere and audio of combat, but also the incapacitation.

Looking at his downed marine, Taylor felt a shiver run up his spine. He had been engaged in several minor conflicts and policing actions around the world, but never had the cause for a real war. Had that been for real, he'd just had lost a marine. He looked up at the casino from around the corner of a shop wall, talking to his team through the throat mics.

"Man down, suspected sniper in the Cortez building, Ortiz and Campbell into firing positions on the tower, everyone else stay low and keep watch!"

"We're getting bogged down, Sir," said Suarez.

"Nothing much we can do about that Lieutenant, we continue the approach and we risk substantial casualties."

"And the longer we wait, Sir, the greater their chance of re-enforcement!"

He sighed, it was yet another far from ideal choice to be making, he was only glad he was not gambling on his men's lives. He peered back around the corner of the shop wall to the tower block of the casino. He grasped his M56 Assault carbine close, a shortened version of the typical caseless ammunition rifle in use throughout the UEN forces. The 8.6mm round had an effective range of four hundred metres and substantial armour penetration for its size.

The training missions did not allow them to make use of their high explosive weapons, artillery or other such destructive means of warfare. However, that meant that it tested their individual combat skills and unit effectiveness to the limit.

"Ortiz and Campbell, continue to setup a firing position, everyone else continue forward."

He jumped out from the shop wall and rushed to the next piece of cover, zigzagging in between rubble, walls and doorways. Their competition would be all too pleased to bag themselves the leading officer early on in the mission. They heard the crack of a weapon firing, quickly followed by one on their own side.

"That's a kill," said Ortiz down the intercom.

"Alright, let's get this shit going! Alpha, first floor breach. Delta, second floor. Bravo and Charlie with me through the ground floor!"

He lifted his rifle and leapt out from cover, upping his pace to an excited dash for the Cortez building. His marines rushed alongside him, the low drum of combat boots droning across the open street. The rest of their equipment made little noise at all, it all being padded and dampened in order to make as little noise as possible. Taylor crashed into the outer wall to the side of the main entrance that was barred shut.

"Ready?"

The men all nodded.

"Breach!" shouted Taylor.

The marines beside him fitted direction charges either end of the doors in the approximate position of the hinges, stepping back quickly to cover from what they knew was coming. All the charges blew simultaneously and the door rocked under the pressure. Finally, with little to hold it in place, it collapsed inwards.

Taylor's two units stormed through the open door as Alpha and Delta squads fired grappling guns up to the first and second floors. The high power rifle-like devices fired a metal anchor that impeded in the concrete wall and expanded within it, hoisting the user quickly upwards under power. He watched as the first few marines soared into the air and smashed through the upper windows.

As shards of glass dropped around him and slid off his helmet, Taylor rushed through the breach into the building. Gunfire rang out in the atrium as he entered the hazy room. Three of the marines of Bravo squad were on the floor and out of action. He looked around, looking for any sign of their enemy.

"Sentry gun, Sir," said Silva.

"Christ, that wasn't part of the training exercise," Suarez said.

Taylor grinned as he let his rifle hang freely on its sling.

"If they made it easy for us then this would be no kind of training exercise at all would it, Lieutenant?"

"This is supposed to be a training exercise for hostage rescue against terrorist and dissident forces!"

"And what would you do when you face terrorists who have got their hands on this sort of equipment? No good whining like a bitch because the enemy aren't playing your game. Get your shit together and act like a marine!"

Suarez looked down, partly in shame and partly in embarrassment. He had just been humiliated in front of half their company. Taylor looked around at his men, several were covering doorways and a stairway, the others were looking on having witnessed the grilling he'd given Suarez. Had he done it to one of them the room would be filled with laughter, but no one dared angering the Lieutenant. Despite this, they were all well entertained, and they'd have a good joke about it later that evening.

"Alpha, report," said Taylor.

"We're in, one casualty from a sensor mine, further devices secure and floor is clear, over."

"Delta, report."

"We're in, no casualties, sweeping floor now, over."

"Four casualties to their one and we're only just through the door. These are unacceptable losses!" shouted Mitch.

He paced up and down the entrance hall of the casino building.

"It's time to move forward, I want section sweeps of every floor. Keep an eye out for any mines, trip wires, sensor devices, traps, anything! These bastards are here to embarrass us and they're doing a damn fine job, it's time to hit back. Bravo and Charlie, up to the third floor, we advance section by section as we secure floors."

The two officers followed on after their marine squads. Mitch knew it was a harsh thing to grill an officer in front of the men, but he also knew how vital it was that they were honed into the best fighting force they could be. Despite not having faced a major war, after hundreds of years of marine combat warfare, he knew it would not be long until their services were needed. Twenty minutes later they were on the eighth floor with no more incidents but neither any sign of their targets.

"Any sign of movement?"

"Motion scanners aren't picking up anything at all, Sir," Baker answered.

"Switch to thermal."

Taylor paced up and down the large room. Many of the gambling tables were still strewn about the place with chips scattered across the floor. It was a sad state to see what was once a highly successful and profitable place.

"Sir, I am getting four readings."

"Four? They've split up?" asked Suarez.

"Or they're using diversions. Either way, we have wasted enough time, we need this extraction stat. Where are the readings coming from, Baker?"

"Looks like, opposite ends of the twelfth floor, north west corner of the fourteenth and south east of the fifteenth."

"A bit scattered aren't they?" asked Suarez.

"That's the idea, they know we need to close this down in a solid time frame. Each of our platoons is only equal to their force, they are trying to even up the odds."

He strolled quickly over to Baker and took the Mappad device from him, studying the readings carefully.

"Alright, Alpha and Bravo take the twelfth floor, Delta the fourteenth, Charlie you're with me on the fifteenth. Remember these guys are slimy bastards, they'll do anything to catch you out. Okay, that'll be all, let's do this!"

Taylor lifted his rifle as he rushed to the steps. He was at the front of the company alongside several of Charlie squad. The heat was still intoxicating, but the shade of the building at least alleviated some of the strain.

They reached the doorway to the fifteenth floor. The entrance was a double door swing system with small windows peering into the hallway. The higher floors were mostly used as a hotel, the fifteenth not being unique in that regard. Taylor carefully moved across the wall until he was beside the doors and peered through one of the windows. It looked onto a long corridor with dozens of doors leading to hotel rooms. Many of the doors were missing or open. He turned back to look at his unit.

"Right, we've got a hotel corridor, perfect spot for an ambush."

Before he could continue the radio cut in.

"This is Alpha, no contact, heat signal was a hoax, over."

They heard an explosion erupt in the floors below.

"This is Bravo, location was booby trapped with a paint bomb, Sir."

"Any casualties?"

"No, Sir, but I guess half of us are out of this mission."

"Send what's left of your platoon to the fifteenth to re-enforce Charlie, over."

Taylor peered back through the window. It was a

peaceful if desolate scene, but he knew better. The British paras were giving them hell that day, and he knew the next step wouldn't be any easier. He turned back to his men.

"Alright, this is likely it, we've taken heavy losses already, I want this finished! Ready on my mark," he lifted his rifle into both hands and took a deep breath. "Go!"

Smashing his foot through the door he rushed in, taking a quick turn into the first doorway. He quickly scanned the room, it was empty. He turned back to see his men running along the corridor. Mitch rushed back out to see Charlie squad swarming through the rooms of the corridor. The radio cut back in.

"Sir, I'm getting different readings, I think they are interfering with our equipment," said Baker.

Taylor watched as his men and the re-enforcements from Bravo squad cleared the floor. They'd been duped, there was nothing there.

"God damn it! I should have known. Fuck the equipment! Let's use some common sense. If you were to hold up in a world class casino and hotel, where would you be?"

"In the penthouse, Sir," said Silva.

"Exactly! Form up, Sergeant, we're heading upstairs, let's end this. Bravo, head to the roof and set up a breach for the penthouse suite, over."

Taylor leapt into a swift stride towards the stairs. Another ten flights in full gear in the heat was gruelling, but the very idea of fatigue had gone from their minds, they were eager to even the odds and set the record straight.

Less that ten minutes later they were waiting outside the entrance to the penthouse. They knew it was the location they had been looking for, they only kicked themselves for not thinking of it earlier. Taylor made a mental note to rely as much on instinct as technology on the future. For all their hardware, they had been deceived.

"This is Bravo, we're good to go."

"All teams, prepare to breach in ten," Taylor ordered.

He looked around to the dozens of marines waiting in the corridor. Several stood next to charges on the walls, others beside the main entrance next to him. All in they had four breach points.

"Three, two, one, breach!"

The explosive charges fired simultaneously and were loud enough that they could not even hear the shattering of glass on the outer of the building as Bravo team swung in from abseil lines. They rushed through the breaches. The residue from the explosions had created a dust and screen throughout the room. Even before Mitch's foot was through the door the guns were blazing.

The ruined old furniture of the luxurious room had been stacked up in make shift defences, the paras really had made maximum use of their numbers and time. So many of the training exercises involved units who put little effort into their resistance, but that was not the case here.

Six marines were dropped on the breach, though Mitch could see at least a few Brits fall as the intensity of their fire increased.

The penthouse was vast, as large as their entire company's quarters on base. They had breached the open plan living and dining area, but there were several doorways leading to other rooms. As the fire continued, the marines were slowly advancing on the positions from both sides. Taylor held point for several of Charlie squad to head for the doorways to his left as he and Sergeant Silva went for the master bedroom.

The two marines slammed up against the wall either side of the door to the bedroom. Taylor looked at his Sergeant and nodded in readiness. Silva reached for the door handle slowly, before quickly ripping the door open. The Major rushed through the entrance with his rifle raised. Initially he could see no sign of life at all, until in his peripheral vision he just caught sight of fast movement. It was too late, a British officer grabbed for his rifle and twisted around until he held his weapon and locked against his chest. The defender was holding him from behind in a tight grasp with a knife at his throat.

Silva entered just a second too late, he raised his rifle to target the attacker but there was little he could do. From the other side of the entrance another Brit was pointing a handgun at the captured Major's head.

"Hard luck, old boy, this day belongs to us," said the

officer.

"Nuts," replied Taylor.

He lifted his offhand and dangled a pin, which had clearly just been drawn from a grenade on his chest rig.

"Oh, shit!" shouted the officer.

The room erupted into a blinding flash of light. The two British soldiers dropped to the ground stunned and disorientated, the two marines stood as if nothing had happened. Taylor stepped over the officer who was rubbing his eyes in a desperate attempt to regain his vision. He was just beginning to get some sight back as Mitch offered out his hand, which the man gladly took.

"Your boys don't have flash protectors yet, Charlie? It's an amazing piece of kit really, a liquified contact lens which increases vision abilities by ten percent while providing a barrier shield against extreme bursts of light."

Taylor hauled him to his feet, a man who had quickly become a friend of over the last three years. Captain Charlie Jones of the British Parachute Regiment, EUA army. Jones shook his head, trying to stabilise his body and regain balance.

"That's a hell of a way to regain control of a situation. It isn't too sporting but if it gets the job done, well!"

"You didn't exactly play it straight yourself, Captain, I lost a lot of men getting up here."

He was glad of the challenge Jones had presented, but aware that had it been for real, they would have experienced far heavier casualties that he'd consider acceptable. The four men went from the bedroom and into the open plan vastness of the penthouse. The mission was over and both sides were hauling fallen comrades to their feet and patting each other on the back.

"What are the total losses, Lieutenant Suarez?"

"Twenty-one casualties, Sir."

Taylor turned to Jones and reached out his hand, which Jones took gladly.

"Good job, Captain, a pleasure training with you once again. All I can say is that I hope we never come out on opposing sides, as it'd be a real meat grinder."

"Agreed."

One of the British soldiers stepped forward to Jones. "Sir, I am getting an urgent request from Commander Phillips to speak with you personally."

"Patch it through to my comm."

"Sir, this is Jones."

The Captain strolled off to the corner of the room, away from the troops. The British and American equipment was largely the same, but what few differences were now masked by the dust that had settled on their gear, making them blend into the demolished room. The men mingled and the ambience grew as they broke out into conversation. Taylor and Suarez stood off to the side of the room watching the men switch from hard-line enemies to the best of friends.

"I am sorry I had to speak to you the way I did, but you must know that it was of the utmost importance. In the field these men rely on our strength and leadership, it is no time to act like a civilian."

"I know, I don't know what came over me."

"I do, you saw the loss of your friends. I know this was a simulation, but I know that you took it hard when you saw it, just as I did. The realisation that had it been for real that we would have just lost many of the men under our command is never an easy one, but it is one that we must accept. You can't win a war without taking casualties, fretting over those already gone will only get more killed, got it?"

"Yes, Sir."

"Good. I know you're a good officer. You have a lot of potential. As long as you can learn to keep a cool head you'll do fine."

Jones strolled back across the room to where the two marine officers were stood.

"All okay, Captain?"

"Not sure. We are being called back to our EU bases immediately. Seems there has been some cause for major concern but nobody is discussing across the airwaves. Our bird has to be in the air within the hour. Sorry to have to leave so soon, Major, but orders are what they are."

"Of course, thank you, Captain. It's a shame we couldn't catch a beer together to finish the day off, but next time."

Jones quickly saluted, waited for Taylor to respond and then turned quickly back to the crowd of soldiers.

"Platoon! Outside, now!" he shouted.

The British paras quickly assembled and were running for the steps, their Captain at the front.

"Sir, I am getting orders to return to base immediately, the Colonel says it is a matter of urgency!" shouted Baker.

"Right, get the birds on the line, we need pickup, stat!"

Baker called in the signal as Taylor turned back to his men.

"Good work here today. We took higher casualties than are acceptable, but we were facing a bastard of an enemy! Next time I want twice as much effort and half as many casualties! We're being pulled back to base on an emergency basis. I have no further information at this time, but I can only imagine the shit that's about to be put before us. Back to the landing zone, now!"

It was less than ten minutes before they reached the point where they were dropped by the copters that morning. They had jogged the whole way back, yet again in the burning sun. It was a relief to see that the birds landing just as they were arriving. They wanted nothing more than to rest their feet and relax in the air-conditioned cabins.

The marines didn't stop on their approach, running directly from the town into the Eagle FVs. It was an hour's ride back to their base, a long haul to be left wondering what was so urgent that required their attention. Many wondered if they had finally been called into a war worthy of their services. There was as much excitement among the men as there was relief at lying back in their seats.

For most of the men it was a welcome break from their early morning mission, but not Major Taylor. He had never been called away in such an emergency before. The fact that their British counterparts had been withdrawn at that exact same moment made him highly suspicious. Something big was going on, he wasn't sure whether to be excited or concerned.

As the copter soared back to base, never lifting more than a few hundred feet above the open plain, the Major got to his feet and went up to the cockpit. The Navy pilot flying the transport was Lieutenant Eddie Rains, a man who to look at lacked discipline. However, years of experience had taught Taylor that Rains was the best pilot he'd met. His ragged appearance and slack manner covered up his courage and abilities.

Rains wore a jumpsuit in the same camouflage pattern that the marines wore, though his sleeves were rolled up. He wore a tattered old desert colour shemagh around his neck. On his front was a shoulder holster that could only be described as a relic. His helmet was decorated with wise cracking quotes from his favourite historical figures. The pilot looked more he'd come from their nations first helicopter war in the 21st century.

"Hey, Sir, how's it hangin'?" Rains asked.

"Good, Lieutenant, fine job on our drop and we appreciate the fast pickup."

"I can take credit for the first, Sir, but the pickup was ordered in no uncertain terms."

"Really?"

"You bet ya. Whatever they want you for, it's big!"

"Any idea what that might be?"

"No, Sir. But the comms have been alive, whatever the news it's mighty big and affects more than just the US of A."

* * *

It was a long journey back to their base for the Major. He now knew that they were heading for big trouble, his imagination could not even begin to get close to the reality of it. A second after they had touched down, Taylor was on his feet and out the door. The landing zone was scattered with aircraft. Just as Rains had suggested, all units had been recalled. Most had already returned, the decks were almost empty. A single jeep was waiting for them with a Sergeant at the wheel.

"Guess we're walking," said Silva.

The driver stepped out from his vehicle and straight up to the officer, saluting quickly but not waiting to be greeted.

"Sir, I am Sergeant Gibbons. I have orders to take you immediately to an emergency assembly of all base officers."

"What about my men?"

"Sir, they'll have to figure it out. This order comes directly from General White."

Taylor nodded. He was surprised at the sheer urgency of the situation, it was beginning to look as bad as he had imagined. Turning back to his men he could already see how pissed off they were at the thought of lugging their kit on foot back to their digs.

"Lieutenant Suarez, get the men back aboard the birds, drop our boys off on the battalion's drill square."

"Sir, that is strictly against base procedures."

"Look around, Lieutenant, there's no one around to give a shit. Get our boys back and put some food in their bellies, I'll return when I can."

He nodded over to the Sergeant who was waiting impatiently. He knew he could not be too stern with his officer, but also that the orders of a General gave him a lot of power. Taylor walked up to the jeep and placed his rifle in the back. He unclipped his armour and felt the immediate release and freedom of its encumbrance being removed.

The jeep was an open top vehicle with a roll cage, running a turbine engine which charged batteries that ran individual motors at each wheel. It was the standard utility of the Marine Corps, being light enough to be slung under their Eagle copters. Many were severely armoured, but not those used as run-arounds on the base or for special mission deployment.

Mitch climbed aboard the jeep and yawned as he sat down. It had been a hell of an early start and the heat was really getting to him. Without saying a word the Sergeant fired up the vehicle and sped off at an unusually fast velocity. The urgency at which Gibbons drove gave yet more indication to the severity of the situation. Taylor bounced ideas around his head about the cause of such drama. He could only think that a major Eastern power was causing trouble. They'd be the only ones capable of causing such concern.

The vehicle pulled up outside the briefing hall. Dozens of cars and jeeps were strewn about the parking lot, with the odd straggler arriving as they did. Taylor leapt from the vehicle and rushed to the door. He still wore his combat fatigues which were covered in dust and sweat patches. He'd never turn out anywhere on the base looking like that, but he had no choice.

Inside the hall he could see it was lined with all the senior officers on base at the time. There was no seating left, so he took up position at the back of the room. There were at least a hundred officers there. At the forefront was a table with three chairs laid out for the General and his staff. Moments later General White and two other senior officers entered the room. They wore their BDUs, meaning they had rushed to the briefing. The audience leapt to their feet as the base leaders sat before them.

"Thank you, Gentleman, be seated," said General White.

The crowd quickly sat down remaining silent. Everyone present was very anxious to hear the news, and the General did not delay.

"Shortly before 0800 hours a distress signal was sent from an Ares colony ship. The message claimed that the base had come under attack by an unidentified enemy. Communication officers on the Moon were unable to regain contact with Ares or its vessels, and based on the contact, there are not expected to be any survivors."

Whispers and comments began to arise across the room, becoming a drowning drone of conversation.

"Pipe down!" shouted White.

They all went silent again.

"Now, based on the information given, we have not been able to identify the attacking forces. The info did not correlate to any military forces that we are familiar with. The crew who sent the message suggested that the forces were not human. Now I don't want anyone to jump to any conclusions. What is clear, is that an advanced enemy has viciously attacked a civilian colony. There are already ships on the way to investigate, but as you know, it'll be months until they arrive."

There was a hush, as no one knew how to take the news. The planet had become used to peace between major powers. A new threat as substantial as was being suggested came as a shock to them all.

"At the moment that is all we know. However, while we should not panic, we must take this threat seriously. Alert levels are being raised across the world and all military personnel are being ordered to base and brought up to combat readiness. For all we know this could be the work of terrorists, an eastern power or a private organisation. Until we know differently, stay calm and be ready. That'll be all."

The General left, but the information he had provided only wetted his audience's appetite. The officers were eager for action, but were still trying to understand and interpret the meaning of what they had been told. Taylor was one of the first to leave. His driver and jeep were gone. He shook his head in surprise, but quickly took to a walking pace, there was nothing left to do but return to his unit.

CHAPTER THREE

Ten days later.

Taylor put his beret on and headed for the door. Stepping out onto the parade ground, Lieutenant Suarez had already gotten the company assembled as ordered. For days they had continued their regime of fitness and combat training. Not another word had been spoken to the Major regarding the urgent assembly with the other officers.

As Mitch walked towards his finely presented unit, a jeep rode into view. Before he could get out a word to the company he recognised the stars below the windshield of the vehicle. It was the General's car. Suarez ordered the men to attention as the vehicle stopped beside them and the General leapt out in an enthusiastic manner. They'd never seen a General move so fast.

"Taylor, with me, now!"

The General had not even broken his stride. He led

Mitch around the corner of the assembly building of the drill square, out of sight and hearing of all who were formed up.

"Sir, what can I do for you?" asked Taylor.

The General turned and took a good look around the area to be sure they were alone.

"This is privileged information, you hear?"

"Yes, Sir."

"The vessels that were dispatched to the Ares colony have been receiving readings of something heading for us. Now we don't know what it is, but it's big. Some experts are saying it's coincidental, but I don't believe in that crap. Official word is that the Ares colony is experiencing communication faults and assistance is en route."

"Sir, that is not at all what we were led to believe."

"Agreed. Whatever is heading our way will be passing the Moon colony first. Now, it's a big colony but has limited military deployment. No order has gone out for us yet, that means my hands are tied. However, that does not stop normal procedure. I am despatching your company to the Moon colony for a training exercise."

"Yes, Sir."

"Let me be clear, officially this is a training mission. Unofficially, we just don't know what to expect. Be sure to take a full armament of live ammunition and all the gear you'll need. I pray that this is all just a misunderstanding, but let us make sure we are ready for anything!"

"Yes, Sir, I'll get on it!"

"I have already cleared you for departure and the stores have been ordered to give all that you ask, they are aware that this is a live fire exercise. You report only to me directly on this, get going ASAP!"

The General nodded in gratitude, he was glad to have officers who he could rely on. He strode off leaving Taylor stood considering his situation. He understood the General would only ask it of him if there were serious danger to the colony. On the other hand he knew that a single company was a meagre force to defend anything.

Walking back to the drill square he stopped in front of his company, the men eagerly awaiting some news. The General's vehicle was already coasting into the distance. He looked around, nobody but his unit in sight.

"Stand easy and come forward!"

The men looked surprised not to be dismissed as per regulations and norm. They huddled around in a circle around the Major. He turned, looking at all their faces.

"We are deploying immediately to the Moon colony. That much is no secret. However, officially we are on a live fire training exercise. Unofficially, I want every one of you on guard and ready to fight. The General has entrusted us with a mission and we will get it done. I want you formed up in one hour, full kit, including counter pressure suits, masks, the lot. Ammunition is on its way. That will be all. Get to it!"

The men initially looked a little dazed, but they quickly snapped out of it as the Sergeants began barking their orders to get the men moving. Suarez moved up to the Major with a puzzled expression on his face.

"What the hell's going on? A few days ago it was high alert, now officially a training mission?"

"Top brass hasn't got a clue what is going on and nobody is keen to give them answers. The General is concerned that we don't sit idle if a threat exists."

"Fine, but one company? If there is any major military threat, what could we even do?"

Taylor turned to him, more than irritated by his constant questions and petty nature.

"A damn sight more than scientists and civilians, that's for sure. Now, kit up, we've got a job to do, Lieutenant!"

Suarez straightened himself realising how foolish he was being. Not only that, he was questioning the orders of his superiors. He saluted quickly before rushing off to gather his equipment. Taylor stood and watched as his company scattered to fulfil their tasks. He was not at all comfortable with their orders.

Through the minor combat and policing actions which the Major had participated, they had always done so with substantial intel. He had little idea what to expect on the Moon colony and that concerned him. Training for immediate deployment was a regular part of their training, so Taylor was glad to see that the entire company was formed up with its gear in thirty-five minutes. They were ready before their transport had even arrived.

The Major paced up and down the square, looking out at his company. They sat about with their equipment stacked in lines, impatiently waiting for the vehicles. Taylor turned to see Sergeant Eleanor Parker walking up to him. He stopped pacing in surprise. He'd always found it difficult to be her superior when they had slept together after more than one operation. Not only that, but she was supposed to be recovering from a broken arm sustained in training.

Parker was shorter and slighter than any marine in the company, but she carried herself tall and proud. Her brunette hair was tied back perfectly and out of sight, her uniform immaculate and with no sign of the arm brace she'd been wearing until the day before. Her blue-grey eyes were piercing, and it was quite clear what she wanted. She quickly saluted and jumped into her request.

"Sir, requesting permission to rejoin the unit for operational duty!"

"Sergeant, you are not cleared from medical leave for another seven days."

"Sir, that's Doctor's recommendations, not orders. I am ready to get back to it. If you have a mission to do you'll need me back."

Taylor looked around the lines of marines. He knew that Parker wasn't fully recovered yet, neither did he want to see any harm come to her. Despite this, he hated the idea of leaving a fellow marine behind. He also knew that she was a useful asset to her platoon.

"Sergeant, no bullshit, can you do your job?"

"Yes, Sir!"

"Alright, fall in, your platoon leader will fill you in on the mission details."

She could not help herself from grinning. She was so happy she could have leapt up and kissed him. For a moment Taylor thought she might even do so.

"That'll be all, Sergeant!"

Parker saluted the Major and immediately heaved her equipment onto her shoulder and joined the rest of the unit. Taylor looked again across the platoons under his command, they were visibly uneasy. No one was being straight about what was expected of them. There was little he could do to remedy that, he knew nothing more himself. Before he could think of any words to calm his troops their buses pulled into view.

"Load up! Let's go!" Taylor shouted.

He watched as his men poured into the vehicles in an efficient and an enthusiastic manner. He commanded five platoons. Four of them were infantry units compromising of forty-one men, and his own sixteen-man command platoon. A Lieutenant led each platoon, with additional officers in his HQ unit. They'd seen more action than any other serving unit in the U.S. military, but that was still nothing compared to the wartime experience of veterans of bygone wars.

The buses coasted on through the base until they could see the assembly area in view. He knew that it would soon be needed for major operational duties, and yet the area was almost empty. A few copters and transports lay unattended and work crews went on leisurely about their jobs. An Achilles transport craft was being loaded and was the only sign of serious work in sight. Taylor could already make out the unmistakeable figure of Eddie Rains guiding in his fellow copter pilots as they loaded up the Falcon shuttles in the cargo bay. The Achilles class transports were the military's main means of transport into space. They could carry up to two hundred and fifty men, and five shuttles.

Thirty minutes later their kit was stowed and they were lifting off. UEN forces did regular training exercises on the Moon, but only a hundred regular troops were stationed there at any time. A further six hundred civilians were part of a colony defence force, citizen soldiers. Taylor knew that his force would effectively double the strength of their numbers, but it was still a fraction of what would be needed against a sizeable enemy force.

Taylor stood on the bridge with his command platoon as they made their break into orbit. The ship was crewed by twenty-four Navy personnel. He grinned as he watched Eddie look in astonishment at their operating procedures. He had no love of their disciplined and machine-like way of working. Captain Reyes commanded the vessel, the Deveron.

"It's an eight hour run, Major, you're welcome to make full use of all the facilities we have to offer."

"Thank you, Captain. I only ask one thing of you. It's important that we discuss our operation en route to the colony. The details of our mission remain top secret. Anything that your crew hear or see must not be repeated to anyone."

"Understood, Sir, those are our standard operating procedures. Loose lips sink ships and all that."

Taylor nodded in agreement and gratitude. He turned to his command staff and signalled for them to follow. He stepped briskly off the deck and straight to the briefing room where all his officers and NCOs were gathered. He was immediately drawn to the sight of Eleanor. He'd not seen her in weeks due to her medical leave, and he could do nothing but admire her, even in her BDUs.

"Quite honestly, we have no idea what to expect. What I can tell you is that it is vital that we remain on guard and armed at all times. That will mean being armed and armoured during all hours that you aren't sleeping."

"Won't that raise some eyebrows with the civilians?" asked Silva.

"It will indeed, Sergeant. Over half a million people live on the moon and they're not used to seeing soldiers in full battle attire. Therefore, officially we are on a training exercise. Our mission entails the practice of colony-wide security and urban navigation and planning."

"It's a bit of a flimsy argument," said Parker.

"It is, but it's the best we have. The government has been ordered to comply so there'll be little in our way other than strange looks and the odd probing question. Stick to the story. All that matters is that we stay on duty and on guard."

"Sir, I have to ask what everyone is thinking. Around a week ago you were called to an emergency meeting, which clearly involved the threat we are now facing. We are being asked to take up defensive measures when we don't know what we're defending against," said Lieutenant Wilson.

Taylor looked at the officer. Wilson led Alpha platoon, a capable leader, one of his best.

"You're right. I will tell you what little I know, because it is of vital nature to this operation. The meeting regarded a message received from an Ares colony shuttle. It alleged that the colony had been attacked by an unidentified and well-armed enemy force."

"What are we talking about here? Aliens?" asked Wilson.

"We simply don't know. What little description we have describes an enemy with technology superior to what we are accustomed to. Top brass isn't willing to jump to any conclusions, and few are willing to entertain the idea of other intelligent life."

"So what, a Chinese force trying to muscle in on the colony? They've been working against the UEN for long enough," said Suarez.

"Possibly, but at this stage we don't know. We have little information to work on and we cannot risk panic by informing the colony of any impending danger."

"What danger, Sir? Why is an attack on Mars relevant to our Moon?"

Taylor dropped his head. He couldn't beat around the bush any longer. He had been tasked on a highly secretive mission, but he could not ask his marines to step into danger without giving them a heads up. He looked back up, staring at each and everyone in the room.

"Okay, Wilson, this is why. Ships were despatched immediately to the Ares colony. As you know it will be months before they can arrive and begin to make sense of what has happened. However, they have picked up signals that something big is heading for Earth."

"What the fuck does that mean, Sir?" Silva asked.

"Some are saying it's a coincidence, an asteroid that'll pass us by. The General does not believe in coincidences and believes we may have trouble. Nobody is sure of anything at this stage and troops cannot and will not be deployed anywhere until there are some rigid facts."

There were so many questions that the officers and NCOs wanted answers to, but clearly no one was able to enlighten them any further.

"I know this puts us in the shit, but we're marines, it's what we're paid for. Our job remains the same. We are to remain on active duty on a permanent rotational basis. All personnel when on duty are to maintain combat attire, as well as full pressure suits and breathing tanks. Keep a full load out of ammo and be ready for anything. When we face the unexpected, we can never have enough ammo. That's all I have to say and the only intel we have to go on."

"One last thing, Sir, the colony is a sizeable city, we are one company, we'll be spread a bit thin?" asked Wilson.

"We'll focus our efforts on the economic centre of the colony only, which includes the government buildings, police headquarters and all key officials. Shuttles will be kept on hand to allow us fast deployment as and when needed. Now, that'll be all. We've got hours to kill, no mission to plan and no training to be done. Your time is your own."

* * *

It was a long and boring journey to the Moon. After the start of their first trip the excitement of being in space and the views from the ship died down. The Major sat on the bridge as they made their descent to the Moon Spaceport. With none of the problems that the Earth's gravity and atmosphere presented, vessels came and went at ease. Mitch had in some ways been hiding from his men. They wanted more answers than he could give, and he was sick of repeating the same story.

It would be a lie for Taylor to say he wasn't scared. Through his intense training and multiple missions on Earth, nothing worried him more than the unknown. In their age of communication and technology, he'd never had to go into a situation as blind as this. Whatever worries he had he couldn't express them, it was his duty above all else to maintain his composure for the benefit of his marines.

"This is it, Major, final descent, you'll be on the ground in three minutes," said Reyes.

"Thank you, Captain, what are your following orders?"

Reyes turned to look at Taylor as if shocked at the question.

"We've been ordered to stay for your duration, Sir."

That bothered Taylor, but said nothing in response. The only reason that the Deveron would be tied up was if the General wanted to be sure they could be evacuated at short notice. It was becoming ever more clear how dangerous the General thought their situation could be. With this in mind, it was more worrying than ever that nobody else appeared to be acting on the information.

"Thank you, Captain, I'll be down below."

Taylor leapt to his feet. He didn't want the crew to see his concern and confusion in the situation. His training was now kicking in, they were about to hit the ground and the only thing he needed to concern himself with was being ready for action. A minute later he was pulling his armour over his compression suit beside his command staff and making final preparations.

"Remember, those are civilians down there, we are there as an emergency measure only, I don't want to cause any more concern than we're already doing. Stay sharp, stay calm, and be ready for anything!"

The Major pulled on his webbing with spare ammunition and the oxygen tank to his back. The magnetic gravity generators first used on the Moon, as well as the oxygen processors, had done wonders in developing the potential for the community. However, as soldiers, they had to be ready for anything. A serious breach in the colony could require them to need both air and their suits.

"Let's move!" shouted Taylor.

He slipped his pistol into its thigh holster, picked up his rifle and strode for the doors of ship. The broad ramp down to the docking bay allowed them to disembark five men wide. The Major was surprised to see that not a single official was present to meet them. For a moment this concerned him, until he had to remind himself that as far as the colony was concerned their presence was only in a benign training capacity. He turned back to his men, who looked just as shocked to find a relatively empty docking bay, the only presence being crews and mechanics.

"Get the birds out, were heading for the LZ immediately!"

The Moon colony was an ugly one, an almost endless expansion of grey structures. There were few windows on the buildings, for without a substantial atmosphere they were always at risk of being struck by space debris. The few small windows that existed were so thick that they distorted any view.

"God, why would you come here by choice?" asked Silva.

"Not our problem, Sergeant."

The fifteen-minute wait for their shuttles was an anticlimactic start to their arrival. For all the mystery of the danger they had been discussing, they half expected to be walking into a battle. It seemed that life went on as usual about the colony. Aside from the stations built on two of the LaGrange Points, the Moon had been the first and only real colony set up outside of Earth. Mars would likely soon follow, as well as many other moons of the Solar System, but not for a few decades.

* * *

Travelling across the Moon city was at least a stress free and easy experience. Most people utilised the solar powered tram network to navigate and commute the area. There was no traffic, no congestion. Having no roads kept things simple and with so little air traffic they had very basic operating procedures for transport.

It was just a ten-minute ride to reach the Civic Centre of the city and the government's own parking facility. No one wore compression suits or oxygen tanks on the colony, unless travelling out of the structures or craft for a specific purpose. They relied on living within atmospherically controlled buildings. Vehicles docked only with sealed dual entry gates and few people ever went outside their artificial environment.

To the marines it was a foreign sight, no crashing seas, mud-ridden fields or craggy mountains. It was not their natural habitat and the more they looked around the less they wanted to be there. Knowing that exposure to the elements could quickly kill a man and that their personal oxygen tanks would only allow survival for half a day or less made it an inhospitable place.

"That's it, Major, not much to look at!" shouted Rains.

Taylor looked through the cockpit screen at the Civic Centre. It was merely a larger version of the ugly buildings that surround it. The shuttles were a bulky and cumbersome transport compared to the fast attack copters that Rains was used to. He didn't like them anymore than Taylor liked the colony.

Minutes later their shuttles docked with the building and Taylor stepped out with his company at his back. Everyone they passed looked at them open mouthed. To see a fully armed and armoured marine was unknown to them outside of the news. Just fifty metres into the building they were met by a sharp-suited man who was certainly an aide to someone important.

"Major Taylor!"

"What can I do for you?"

"Sir, I am James Dallah, the Prime minister has asked me to attach myself to your unit during your stay."

"Good, then you can put out a message for me."

Taylor tried to continue his stride through the building but the arrogant Dallah put his hand out and stopped the Major. Taylor looked up in disgust at the arrogant little man, but he knew he could not risk a political incident at this stage. Had it been back on base he'd have struck the man down where he stood.

"Dallah was it? Don't ever touch me again. Get the Commander of UEN forces to a meeting with me, and make it happen within the hour!"

James looked up at the Major who was an imposing figure, and at the endless stream of fully equipped marines behind him. He nodded, but before he could answer the loudspeaker running through the building rang out.

"Major Taylor, please report to the Prime Minister's Office immediately. Major Taylor to the Prime Minister's Office."

"Guess word travels fast," said Suarez.

"I will lead you to him, please follow me, Major," said

Dallah.

Taylor turned to his men.

"Captain Friday, take up positions throughout the facility, make sure we have men on every floor and at all entrances. Price and Kwori with me."

"Yes, Sir."

The Major followed the snivelling ministerial aide through the corridors of the building as his marines scattered throughout. The Captain was a quiet man, but eminently capable in any situation and had Taylor's full confidence. Dallah led the Major and his men into an elevator and up several floors to what were clearly the most elaborate facilities of the building, which was not saying much.

Taylor was continually amazed at how Spartan the Moon colony was. As a marine he was used to roughing it, but his officer's quarters could only be described as luxurious compared to what he was seeing now. Dallah opened the doors to the secretary's office that led to the Prime Minister's office. Two policemen were posted outside and armed with handguns, a lax security compared to what their Earth officials would expect.

Taylor nodded to his two marines, signalling for them to take up positions outside beside the policemen. The guards looked uneasily at the armoured marines. It was their colony policy to not have military personnel in state buildings, let alone with the kind of hardware they were carrying. The Major could see that the officers were desperate to interrupt and stop him entering with a rifle slung across his chest, but they were under orders not to.

Dallah pulled open the doors. The Prime Minister was stood looking out of a thick porthole across the colony. Two men were sitting at his desk, both wearing military uniform. Taylor went through into the office in full battle attire. The Prime Minister turned to greet him, but surprisingly was not at all shocked by his hardware. He nodded to Dallah to shut the door and leave.

"Major Taylor, this is Commander Kelly of the Moon Defence Force, and Colonel Visser of the UEN. I have called you here because we have just received some troubling news, but it would appear you were better informed than any of us," said Prime Minister Olsen.

"Information has been withheld from us, Major, and that is unacceptable," said Visser.

"Gentleman, you can complain all you like, but I am a soldier, not a politician. My only concern is the safety of the colony and its people, so let's cut to the chase."

"You think you can come in here and treat is like dirt?" shouted Kelly.

"Calm down the lot of you," said Olsen.

"Major, we've just been informed by the UEN President that a large object, which appears to be a space vessel, is on a direct path to us and Earth. Also that they have lost contact with the fleet sent to investigate what they called an 'incident' on Mars. What can you tell us?"

"Clearly you now know as much as I do. I suggest you call all soldiers and territorials to arms, we may well have a fight on our hands."

"A fight? With who and why?"

"I honestly don't know, Colonel. Whoever is on the way has already attacked a civilian colony and has made no attempt at communication. We can only assume that they will continue with hostile actions."

A light began to flash on the Prime Minister's intercom. He quickly tapped the open channel button for hands free.

"What is it?" he snapped.

"Sir, I have a General White on the line for you."

"Put him through!"

"Prime Minister, I am Major Taylor's commanding officer and will be your contact from now on."

"Go on, General."

"What we suspect to be a vast ship heading your way is a concern, but no longer our first concern. It appears that a smaller vessel has split away and is heading for you at a far greater speed."

"What are you saying, General? Give it to us straight."

"Information is still sketchy, but it would appear the main vessel is coming for Earth and this smaller ship to your colony. As a military man, I'd have to say that it is typical of an attack vector."

"We are talking about a mass scale attack, by who?"

"We simply don't know. We have not seen anything like the size of these ships before. Nor are we aware of any technology which would allow vessels to travel that fast, not even our fastest craft."

"I am lost for words, General."

"Then let me tell you the only thing you can do. Break open your weapons, ensure every man and woman who is capable is armed and ready. We don't know what to expect, but we do know it's hostile and bearing on us quickly!"

"Even with your Major's men we could not muster a thousand soldiers, surely not enough for any kind of defence. What about evacuation to Earth?"

"Negative, with the size of your population and time we have, you wouldn't be able to get out more than ten percent of the colony. Based on our last estimates, you've got about six hours."

"Christ, how could it come to this?" Kelly asked.

"Thank you, General, I'll assemble our forces immediately."

"Good luck, Prime Minister."

The line switched off and Olsen looked at the others with utter shock about his face.

"Sir, we have to start now," said Taylor.

"Yes, yes I understand. Form all troops immediately, I'll leave the details to you men."

"Commander, Colonel. You surely have a lot of work ahead of you, with your permission I should see to my own men and get them ready."

"Get to it, Major," said Kelly.

Taylor rushed out of the room, nodding to his two marines on the way out to follow him. He didn't even break stride to say a word to them. The Major was shaking his head in dismay. It was obvious that this sort of threat existed days ago and the authorities did nothing. In that time they could have deployed several divisions to the Moon or evacuated the entire colony to the safety of Earth. He tapped his intercom.

"Taylor to Deveron, come in, over."

"This is Deveron, over."

"I need a direct line to General White, can you organise that for me?"

"Sir, he is already waiting to speak with you."

"Put him through."

The Major continued to stride through the vast Civic building as he was put through to the General.

"Major Taylor, you're about to be hit by a shit storm, we both know that. We also know that if you are faced with any serious force you'll never hold out."

"Yes, Sir."

"Your orders are simple, your number one priority is Prime Minister Olsen. He knows a tremendous amount about Earth's governments, its workings, strengths and security. He is a major asset to any enemy. You are to protect him at all costs. If possible, in situ, if that proves impossible, evacuate immediately. If there is any risk of him falling into enemy hands, you put two in the chest and one in the head. Do I make myself clear?"

"Absolutely, Sir, and the rest of the civilians?"

"You have your orders, Major. Protect the Prime Minister, bug out if need be. The most valuable assets to us are the Prime Minister's life and the men at your command!"

The Major looked around to be certain that no one other than his marines could hear as he was horrified at what he was hearing.

"Sir, you want us to leave the civilians and UEN forces to die?"

"Taylor, get this into your head. Big shit is going down, potentially world changing. Tough times call for tough measures, you do what you have to do, more importantly, what you're ordered to!"

"Affirmative!"

"Okay, keep me in the loop, over and out."

Taylor reached Captain Friday and Lieutenant Suarez who had set up a command post in one of the quiet offices of the ugly and utilitarian building. He pulled back a chair and slumped into it with a sigh.

"What is it, Sir?" asked Suarez.

Taylor looked up at his officers, five of his command staff were present.

"Shut the door."

Captain Friday did as ordered, in his usual silent and efficient manner.

"We aren't here to safeguard the population. Our orders solely revolve around Prime Minister Olsen. His protection is our only concern. If we cannot protect him here, we are to pull out evac him to Earth immediately."

"And just leave everyone behind?"

"Fact is, Suarez, if it gets to that point, there won't be much we do can for them."

The room went silent. None of them could believe that they were being asked to leave civilians behind in the case of disaster.

"I know it sucks, but it's our job. Now, I want the Deveron docked on the roof of this building. Officially it'll be there to act as a static gun defence, which will at least in part be true. It will also be ready for an immediate bug out should we need it. We've got a few hours, get the men on rotation and make sure everyone gets at least a couple of hours kip. With any luck there'll be no fighting at all, but let's be prepared for the worst."

* * *

Hours had passed with little rest for any involved. Major Taylor stood beside the Prime Minister as they watched the hulking vessel approach. The communications officers continued to put out signals in multiple languages, as well as light and sound communication. They had received no response. Mitch tightened his grip around his gun, he had a bad feeling about what they were about to face.

The Prime Minister and all other key command staff were in the emergency command and control centre that was built below the surface of the Civic Centre. It was intended to be a centre for use during environmental disasters or internal threats to the safety of officials. All watched open mouthed at the monitors as the huge vessel soared towards them.

The vessel was the size of a city. You would be hard pressed to explain its actual shape with so many protruding structures that appeared to be fins and aerials. The finish of the vessel was harsh and industrial, as if it was bare ironwork in a factory. It was an ugly ship in every way, but no less imposing. It was elongated with vast engines at its rear and an aggressive and ugly prow resembling a hammerhead shark.

"They're three miles out, Sir."

"I don't want anyone showing any aggressive action at all, let's not provoke a war," said Olsen.

They watched in amazement as a huge door opened on the mouth of the vessel, though it was small in scale to the ship. The space glimmered as camouflaged ships poured out in their dozens.

"Look at that, the way they blend into space," said Kelly.

"Yes, a chameleon camouflage technology, something

we never managed to develop to an operational standard. You don't use such devices when you come in peace," replied Taylor.

"Easy, Major, let's not jump the gun."

"Sir, our comms are being jammed, we've gone dark," said Visser.

"Prime Minister, this is an attack, do not let them invade unopposed!" shouted Taylor.

"Major Taylor, must I remind you who is in charge!"

"Gentleman!" Kelly shouted.

They turned to see the craft descending on their colony. It was impossible to make out the total number as their camouflaging technology meant that they were difficult to spot and count, but it was already at least fifty.

"We must find some way to make contact," said Olsen.

"Can we access any of the video feeds, Commander?" asked Taylor.

"Only from cameras in and on this building which are connected directly, all others are jammed along with comms."

They heard a loud striking noise as one of the unidentified vessels landed against the side of the civic building. There was silence for several seconds as every person in the room anxiously awaited their next action.

"I need to investigate that personally, keep the blast doors shut and only open them when I return!" Taylor ordered.

"Major, this could be a first contact situation, I must be there!"

"Sit down, Prime Minister! Everything we know and have seen so far suggests the actions of a hostile force, you will go nowhere near them until I am satisfied!"

Olsen dipped his head. He was angry for being put in his place, but he knew how foolish he was being. It was potentially a very exciting time and he was letting it get the better of him.

"Alright, Major, investigate, but do not in any way show aggression."

"Yes, Sir."

The Major hit the large button that opened the broad blast doors and stepped out. The foot-thick doors sealed behind him. In front of him stood Lieutenant Wilson and the whole of Alpha platoon, as well as half of his command section.

"Alpha with me, the rest of you, do not let anyone pass but me, I don't care who they are!"

Taylor took his rifle firmly in both hands and led the platoon directly for the area where they'd heard the ship land. A moment later they could hear heavy cutting equipment being used and a few screams of panic as staff members ran in fear of the harrowing sounds. Their civic building was being breached. Taylor had no idea who the enemy might be, but he knew firmly that they were not the actions of a peaceful people.

A thud rang out as a section of the thick outer wall fell in and collapsed onto the floor. Taylor got up to a jogging pace, making his way as quickly as possible to the breach. Before they could arrive, the strangest sounds began pulsating around the rooms.

The marines could hear screams from the vicinity of the breach. At a corner up ahead they saw a person hit with some kind of red energy which appeared to burn into their flesh causing them to drop to the ground in agony, clearly fatally hit. Taylor turned to look at his men who had a mix of shock and fear about their faces. He could hear several heavy footsteps coming down the corridor towards them.

"Wilson, take half your men back the way we came and flank their position, we'll hold up here."

"Rules of engagement, Sir?"

"Shoot the bastards, all of them!"

Wilson nodded and quickly peeled off half the men from their group. Taylor signalled for the men to take up defensive positions. He had just over twenty men and no cover at all in the long corridor. All he could do was bring all their weapons to bare and hope that they could destroy whatever came around the corner.

Just a few doors were open along the corridor, but they were of little use as the rooms were all enclosed. If they couldn't take them in the open then they'd have no choice but to run. The marines took up position like a musket block from an 18th century war, bunched up and with no shelter.

The tension was like nothing they had ever experienced as they awaited an enemy they had never seen and knew nothing about. The footsteps were a walking pace but loud. Taylor held his carbine at the ready, a high power, sixty-round capacity assault rifle. They had two machine gunners with them with the BRUN light support guns. The back mounted ammunition with direct feeds to the weapons not only made them a formidable sustain fire weapon, but also balanced them rearward so they could be fired from the hip and on the move using the helmet-mounted sighting system.

The time for wondering was over. A huge metal clad monster came into view. It was almost as tall as the ceiling. They could see little but metalwork. The lower body tapered strongly into a form of sprung legs that made it walk more like the pre-historic dinosaurs. Two arms extended from its upper body and held a huge cannon dwarfing anything the marines could carry. No head sprouted from the top of the armoured suit, only a mirrored dome in the centre of the shoulder line. They could only imagine that whatever was inside was peering through the mirrored section at them.

Taylor looked once more at the imposing metal beast standing over the body of its latest victim. He gave no orders and just pulled the trigger. A split second after firing the first round he was joined by the other marines. The iron beast was slowly knocked back by the mass of fire. It tried to turn its weapon to fire but the cannon was struck by multiple hits. One shot fired off, burning through a sidewall.

Finally the heavily armoured monster slumped against the far side wall and collapsed into a heap. Taylor got to his feet and moved cautiously towards the daunting thing. He guessed they must have fired a couple of hundred rounds into the target. Despite not knowing how many were necessary to destroy the beast, it was becoming quickly apparent that they were facing a vastly superior enemy.

Reaching the end of the corridor, Mitch peered around the corner, finding nothing but the bodies of two more civilians. He looked down at the lifeless armoured suit, most of their rounds had bounced right off the thick armour. The suit was in many ways crude and industrial, riveted and bolted together. He could see a handful of entry points where their bullets had penetrated, all in the thinner joint areas and the mirrored section. A blue liquid seeped from the holes in the suit, he had no idea whether it was blood or some fluid from the suit. Gunfire rang out from the other end of the floor from Wilson and his marines. The Major spun around to look at his men who were anxiously waiting for orders.

"Whatever these things are our rifles can only penetrate their armour at the joints and at that mirrored section.

When you face another, choose your targets carefully. Our grenade launchers will hopefully do more damage, but we can't risk their use here, a breach in the structure of the building could be detrimental. Sergeant Silva, send runners out through the building, we are getting the hell off of this rock."

"Sir, what about the Prime Minister?"

"I'll take the men of Alpha here, less any runners you need. Set your watches for a fifteen minute countdown, anybody not at the boat by then gets left behind."

"Yes, Sir."

Taylor stormed back the way he'd come. Silva peeled off three of the marines as they went, the rest following after the Major. He'd not been without communication links since his blackout training years before. He continued onwards at the head of the marine unit. Based on the size of the vessel that breached the building and the size of the thing that attacked them, he speculated that there would likely be no more than ten intruders in the building.

Minutes later the Major stormed into the hallway before the blast doors of the Prime Minister's bunker. His command staff stood with their rifles ready to fire, they were highly-strung and ready to shoot. He walked straight past them and up to the camera beside the doors.

"This is Major Taylor, get these doors open!"

Seconds later the huge blast doors slid open and he went into the bunker. The occupants were in shock, having watched civilians being gunned down on camera.

"Prime Minister Olsen. The colony has been compromised, we cannot defend it any longer with the few troops we have, I have orders to evacuate you immediately!"

Olsen did not answer for a few seconds, still traumatised by the incident.

"The Prime Minister will not leave his colony, this is our home!" Kelly shouted.

"It's not up for discussion, those are my orders. There's space for anyone here who wants to join us. Sir, please come with us now."

Colonel Visser reached for his handgun, but Taylor lifted his rifle and took the officer in sight. His marines moved into the bunker beside him, outnumbering the guards in the room.

"You cannot remove the Prime Minister without his permission!"

"You do what you have to do, Colonel, but I'm working on orders from General White. The colony will be overrun in the next few minutes, if we do not go now we may never make it out!"

"And what about the people of this colony?"

"What we can do for them is get you out and to safety, Prime Minister. Your death will not help them in any way. Sir, come with us."

The Prime Minister staggered forwards, the walk of a

man who had lost everything. Visser released his grip on the pistol on his belt and relaxed.

"Colonel, Commander, you coming or not?"

"Sorry, Major, but I have a sworn duty to protect this colony," said Kelly.

The Colonel nodded in agreement with him. "You get the Prime Minister to safety and make sure you give them hell, we'll do what we can here."

The Major turned and led Olsen out of the bunker.

"Form up, we're moving out!"

The marine unit rushed to the elevators that would take them right up to the docking area of the Deveron. Gunshots echoed around the building. They could not tell whether it was their own marines or the other soldiers stationed there, but they could no longer concern themselves with it. They crammed into the elevators. Taylor kept the Prime Minister close at all times.

It was a thirty-second journey to the upper floor, but it felt much longer. As they approached the top floor they could hear the sound of gunfire getting louder. It quickly became apparent that their fellow soldiers were already engaged in combat outside the docking bay.

The doors slid open and Alpha platoon burst out into a warzone. Eight marines lay dead or dying on the floor, the rest were battling ferociously against five of the armoured attackers. The beasts made no attempt to use any cover. The room had tall ceilings and was a broad open docking area. A few crates on the bay floor were all that provided cover against the onslaught of the beasts.

Taylor left the elevator firing repeatedly. Within seconds of them arriving, his half of Alpha platoon brought down a creature. Seconds later they were joined by Charlie who came up from the stairs. Almost a hundred marines fired repeatedly. Five more of them were hit as the metal beasts toppled to the ground.

Looking around at the docking bay area, Taylor was astonished at the hardship they'd faced. Even when outnumbering the invaders substantially they had taken severe fatalities, including many others wounded. He could smell burning and was drawn to the smouldering on his shoulder. One of the enemy shots had skimmed his shoulder and upper arm protection. It had burnt it down to the layer of his compression suit.

"All aboard! Immediate evac!" he shouted.

Taylor took Prime Minister Olsen's arm personally and pulled him across the docking bay. The marines hauled their fallen and wounded comrades onto their shoulders dragging them through the docking doors of the Deveron. They were met by Captain Reyes who was armoured up and limping from a shot that had skimmed his leg.

"Get us the hell out of here, Captain, and make sure you man the guns, we'll need everything we've got to make it off this rock!"

"All aboard, Major?"

"We can't wait any longer Captain!"

Reyes hit his intercom as the marines rushed in through the narrow docking corridor.

"Ensign, prepare for lift-off in twenty seconds!"

"Come on, marines! Move your ass!" shouted Taylor.

The last men leapt aboard as the engines fired up and the Captain shut the docking door and released the corridors. Taylor followed the hobbling Captain to the elevators that led them directly to the bridge. He looked out at the colony, a surprisingly peaceful sight considering the slaughter going on within the structures.

"If they wanted us all dead why didn't they just carpet-bomb the colony?" asked Reyes.

"No idea, Captain. Right now, I don't care. Put everything to the engines that you've got, we need to move!"

"Already done, Major."

They quickly soared to a height and were well on their way to Earth. It was fortunate that the Deveron was one of the fastest space-going vessels in usage, as no civilian craft could come close to matching its performance.

"Sir, we've got four ships closing on us fast!" called the Ensign.

"Have we got gunners in position?"

"Yes, Sir."

"Tell them to fire at will!"

"Captain, whatever you have, mines, bombs, anything, you need to use it," said Taylor.

"Sir, I'm having problems tracking them, I can barely make them out on screen!"

The Major and the Captain looked at the live feed of the ships closing in on them, barely more than a glimmer in space. The chameleon technology they used was both magnificent and frightening to watch. The rail guns began to fire, the first few hits did little to deter the attackers but moments later one was hit hard and erupted, its chameleon skin flicking off and they watched silently as it scattered into space in a thousand pieces.

A beam of light surged from the lead vessel and struck their hold, violently shaking the ship. An emergency red beacon began to flash as it become apparent that they had a breach.

"Take them out, Captain, now!"

"Deploy mines on a scatter pattern, everything we have!" shouted Reyes.

Seconds later the enemy craft were enveloped by a scattershot of mines which erupted on impact. The craft were obliterated, leaving nothing more than unrecognisable residue. The bridge crew erupted with ecstasy at their victory.

"Seal that breach, get repair crews down there immediately! We'll need to be patched up for entry into Earth atmosphere in six hours!" Reyes ordered.

"That it? We free and clear?" asked the Major.

"It would appear so, Sir."

"Good, keep me notified of any contact on the scanners."

CHAPTER FOUR

Arriving back on Earth was not quite the victory parade that any of them had imagined, but it was a relief to be back in a hospitable atmosphere and amongst a sizeable military force. They landed outside the Military Hospital where medics were waiting them to help them. They had fourteen killed and nineteen wounded. Major Taylor walked down the ramp to be met by General White as the medical orderlies carried and assisted the injured. The General smiled at seeing the Prime Minister with the Major.

"Good work, Major. As you can imagine we need an immediate debrief, have your men get food, and then re-supply immediately. The base is on Alert One, all combat troops to remain armed at all times."

"Good work? We've come back with our tail between our legs, Sir."

"You made a tactical withdrawal in the face of superior odds, Major. Now please, follow me, both of you."

Taylor nodded to Captain Friday to carry out the orders he'd overheard and proceeded to follow the General, climbing aboard his command car with the Prime Minister remaining at his side. Riding through the base the atmosphere was a far cry from what they'd known before departing. There was no larking about, no games being played, no fitness training. A serious tone had swept across the men and women of the base. They all went about cautiously with a weapon close to hand.

General White's driver pulled up outside the briefing hall where he'd first heard about the troubles just over a week ago. The last thing he expected was to be returning there with news of an alien invasion and a number of his company dead or wounded. Taylor had always hoped he would handle himself well in a combat situation, but this was not a real test of the theory.

Reading combat reports he'd found many accounts of officers freezing under pressure or getting their men pointlessly killed. His first real test had been in far from favourable circumstances, despite carrying out his mission exactly as ordered. It was not what he would call a successful mission. Losing men and women he had trained with weighed heavily on him. He wanted to swear he'd not lose another, but he also knew it was not how a war could be fought.

Security outside the briefing hall was higher than ever, but not just with base personnel. Security from the UEN forces as well as Eastern soldiers and plain clothed security guarded the perimeter.

"What is this, Sir?"

"An emergency gathering. We've got all the major key players here."

Mitch had hoped for something a little more low key, but he knew it was too much to hope for. He stepped off the jeep, still wearing his full armour and with weapon in hand. He'd ordered his men to stay in full battle attire until the end of the mission. They had witnessed enough of the unexpected to be caught with their pants down.

He threw his rifle back into the jeep, content in the knowledge that he was in a safe position. He still maintained a handgun on his body, in keeping with the base security condition now in place. None of the security guards, in uniform or not, made any attempt to question him on entry, knowing rightly not to stand in the way of General White.

The room had been hastily set up in a round table layout. Unlike the crowded briefings he was used to, less than fifty people were in there. They were deep in conversation, but went silent upon his entry. The General led Taylor right up to his own seat and addressed the room.

"This is Major Mitch Taylor, from the mission previously discussed. Major, before you are Presidents,

Prime Ministers, Generals and envoys from all the major countries and joint forces in the world. We will take a full briefing later, but please, give us a concise overview of the enemy."

Taylor looked around the room as they all stared back at him. He had addressed crowds on a regular basis in his career, but faced with the cutting silence and having to address the most powerful men and women of the planet, was daunting. His mouth was dry, but finally he found his words.

"The unidentified enemy made no attempt at communication, nor responded in any way in the attempts we made. They attacked relentlessly. Their smaller ships use a type of chameleon camouflage tech. Their ships, both large and small, are faster than anything we have in space. Their soldiers wear heavily armoured suits which stand over two metres tall and use some kind of energy weapons which burns through the best of our armour at close range."

He looked again at them all, but there was no response, no questions.

"Our small arms could only damage the enemy in a few number of weak points. Based on what I have seen, they intend to conquer our entire civilisation. I saw no mercy, no intention to enslave our people or take hostages. They are coming for us."

The room was still eerily silent as everyone tried to

digest the difficult information they were being dealt. Finally the President of the United States stood up.

"Thank you, son, you've done a fine job. I'd hope we'd not need you for further combat duties, but I am sad to say it is almost certain that we will. Be sure to provide the General with any recommendations on equipment and I will do my best to get it supplied on an emergency basis."

"Thank you, Mr President."

"That'll be all, Major, please see to your wounded and be ready for a full debrief when I am done here," General White ordered.

Taylor saluted and strolled back out of the room, leaving the Prime Minister with the rest of the delegates from around the world. Stepping out into the daylight he was greeted by a most unexpected sight, Captain Charlie Jones.

"Major, you look like hell!"

Neither man saluted the other. They were beyond the point where either felt it was necessary. Their countries' regulations did not strictly require it of foreign personnel either. Instead the Major outstretched his hand in friendship. The British Captain studied his burnt armour in surprise.

"What are you doing here, Captain?"

"Additional security detail for Brigadier Dupont of the EUA. So they gave you a hard time I hear?"

"They? Haven't we got a name for them yet?" asked

Taylor.

"Well our intelligence is still lacking. The word 'aliens' is floating around the base, but none of the top brass is keen to entertain the notion. Many are still holding onto the idea of it being some terrorist or extreme faction on Earth that is trying to flex its muscles."

"Not a chance, you should have seen them, Charlie. They resemble nothing that exists on Earth or any of our bases and colonies."

"Word has it there's a far larger force en route for us, any idea how long they'll be?"

"Based on what I've seen, we've got a few days at most until their main force gets here."

"Christ, so we could be war before the week is out?"

"Sorry, Charlie, but you'll have to excuse me, I've got a number of wounded that I need to call on before the General starts his debrief."

"Of course, good to see you made it out."

Taylor nodded and continued on to the General's jeep. He climbed aboard, much to the surprise of Sergeant Gibbons.

"Take me back to the hospital, Sergeant."

The man tried to turn and argue with the Major, but when he made eye contact with Taylor it became clear that it would be folly. If nothing else, the officer looked ready to strike him if he didn't do as ordered.

Visiting the wounded was a painful experience for

Taylor, not only having to see men he considered friends in pain, but to know that many more would follow them when they went back into action. He could see that many officers and politicians still believed that they could avoid war, but he knew already that it was a conflict they could not avoid.

The rest of the day was spent in a briefing room with General White and several other staff. They went over the same events time and time again. The reality was that he did not have much more to say than he'd said hours before to the worldwide delegates. There was nothing he could say to them to convey the spine chilling evil that the enemy invoked. At every opportunity the interrogators tried to find a way to support their theory that they were mere humans with advanced and experimental technology.

Finally Taylor was released to go back to his quarters to rest for the night. The base was still on high alert and that meant guard duties for all units on base, with double security at the entry points. He staggered into the officers' block. The tall apartment building housed all the officers of his battalion. Their individual homes were a decadent luxury compared to the accommodation of the rank and file. He tapped in his security code to the entry pad and went into his hallway. He stopped abruptly to at the sight of the lights being on. Even if he had left them on, they automatically shut off an hour after leaving the room empty.

The Major's hand reached quickly to his handgun and drew it into a two-handed grip. Adrenaline flowed through his body and his heart pounded. After the frightful slaughter he'd witnessed on the Moon colony, the thought of his own home being invaded was deadly. He took the bend around the hallway leading to his living room, quickly snapping around the corner with his pistol held ready to fire.

Fearing the worst, he was met by Parker sitting on his sofa with a cold beer in her hand. He sighed as he lowered his pistol, realising that his paranoia would soon lead to a heart attack. The beautiful Sergeant was still wearing her BDU trousers tucked into her bulky combat boots. She wore a tight fitting tank top, hugging her toned body. She looked like she'd come right from a day's work, but had let her lightly curled hair down over her shoulders. She sipped back on her beer casually and finally spoke as he stood speechless.

"Not here to kill you, Major."

He lowered his pistol and slipped it into the holster fitted to his leg. He knew that it was as romantic a gesture as he'd ever see from Eleanor. There were no candles, no mood lighting and no fancy music. He didn't mind though, he simply didn't have the energy to put up with such complexities.

"You know this is a bad idea, Sergeant?"

"Yes, Sir," she replied.

"And yet you're still here?"

"The world's going to shit, Sir. We'll probably be in combat within days, may as well make the most of the free time we have."

Taylor relaxed and felt his shoulders lower slightly as his body accepted there was no longer any danger, at least in the form of an attacker. He went over to the fridge and opened the door, looked at what little it contained. He reached for a beer, but as he did so he felt Parker's hands on his back, wrapping around his body. He knew it was a mistake to fraternise with anyone he worked with, let alone an NCO, but he was too tired to care about the dangers.

Turning to look into her eyes, he knew she was right about enjoying their last moments of peace. They had just a few hours before all hell would break loose. He took her in his arms, instantly forgetting all his woes and worries.

* * *

The next day was even more anxious than the last. Sensors were reporting that the vast ship they had detected from the beginning was closing fast on Earth. The vessel that attacked the Moon colony had disappeared, with experts widely predicting that it had put down on the Moon to continue their conquest of the colony. The LaGrange star bases had been hastily abandoned after the Moon colony disaster, with the tens of thousands of inhabitants arriving at major star ports across the planet. For all of humanity's drive for the stars, they once more found themselves running back for Earth.

The Major was called to a briefing soon after breakfast, the General's driver was sent to pick him up, something he was becoming familiar with. He entered the briefing room to find twenty officers. The lowest rank in the room was a Colonel, but most wore stars about their uniform. This was a gathering of some of the most significant leaders of the country.

"Major Taylor, we have gathered here the leaders of almost all forces on the western seaboard, as well as representatives from east coast bases, Canada and the South America Union," said General White.

Mitch stepped forwards to where they sat. There was no operations table, no scattering of intelligence information, simply a meeting of the minds. He looked at the almost empty table in surprise.

"As you can see, Major, we have little information to work on. Your first hand experience of this new enemy is all we have to go on, take a seat."

As Taylor sat down the General hit a button bringing up a large screen at the far end of the table, with a map of the world displayed. Across it were listed the approximate quantity of troops, armour and ships across all countries of the globe.

"As we speak, every military and paramilitary force in the world is calling up troops to operational status. We will of course attempt to avoid war at all costs. The world has been ravaged by enough world wars, another could well be the end of us all."

Another man spoke up, his uniform showed that he was a Lieutenant General.

"Son, we need to have some understanding of what to expect here and you are the highest ranking officer to have fought and survived this enemy. Based on what you have seen, and the intel we have shown you about the size of the vessel approaching, what would you expect them to do?"

"Major, this is Lieutenant General Smith."

"General, I know you by reputation. Sir, I'm a ground officer, tactics for vast scale invasion are a long way from my understanding."

"Please, just indulge us, Major."

"Well, Sir, they aren't a subtle enemy. They are big, bulky, well armoured and very aggressive. Their chameleon ship camouflage should not make you think they are stealth opponents. At the Moon colony they simply orbited with a carrier type vessel and began a ground assault the second they had arrived."

"And what would you draw from that, Major?"

"I would expect much the same, on a much larger scale. The vessel that attacked the Moon colony was a fraction of the size of what's heading for Earth. If they have the technology, I'd expect this huge vessel to break into Earth's atmosphere."

"Why?"

"It's what I'd do, the atmosphere makes supply lines difficult to handle when carrying out a ground attack. If they can get these huge vessels into our atmosphere they will have constant access to carrier vessels, ammunition, personnel."

"Major, our scanners show that this vessel is quite frankly vast, likely as large as many substantial countries."

"I appreciate that, Sir, but we have to stop thinking about what is possible with our technology and start thinking what would we do if we were a hundred years ahead."

The room went silent for a moment as the top brass were left speechless. Several poured water into glasses to clear their dry throats. Another General spoke up, he was wearing a Canadian uniform.

"Let's just be certain about this, nobody is saying what this new enemy is. We don't know where they have come from, they have technology far superior to our own and they have avoided or an unable to make contact with us. Nobody has yet called them anything but an enemy. Seems to me that we are talking about here is a foreign enemy, in other words, aliens."

There was yet another uncomfortable silence as

each and every one of thought about what they had all been wondering. It was preposterous for senior military personnel to believe in aliens. For centuries writers and moviemakers had fired the imaginations of people around the world with such wild and fantastical stories. However, they could not avoid the facts before them.

"Having witnessed this enemy first hand, I can say with every confidence that they can only be an alien life form," said the Major.

"Okay, well at least we can agree to that, but what do we call the bastards?" asked White.

"Well, Sir, the name that's floating around in my company is Mechs. The suits they appear to wear are crude mechanical devices, they joke about them being like the Ironclads of the Civil War."

"Mechs? Well it's a better name than anyone else can come up with."

"If these so called Mechs do intend to enter our atmosphere as you predict, Major, where would they go with something so vast?"

"Well we still do not know the extent of their technology, they may have a means of keeping that hulk in the air. At this stage, General, your guess is as good as mine."

General White got up from his chair and paced around the room behind the seats. He rubbed his chin and scratched his baldhead.

"Seems to me like we're no further forward on

understanding our enemy. Major, thank you for coming in. Keep your men on alert, we may well have work for you."

Taylor stood up and saluted. He was glad to walk out of that room. A meeting with top brass was never a comfortable experience, and that had been the worst he had experienced. He knew that everything he said would be submitted to the President and all key officials. They were relying on him as an advisor, and yet he had very little to say.

Above all, the Major was afraid of this new enemy. Everyone feared the power, technology and mystery of the new foe, yet nobody was willing to admit it publically. He knew that a massive weight was being laid on his shoulders. No matter what happened over the coming days, he would always be called upon as a key commander in this new war of epic proportions.

Stepping out of the building, Mitch looked around the base. Eagle FVs passed overhead alongside fighter aircraft. There was a constant air presence over the base and a ten-kilometre radius. Armoured personnel carriers rolled around the roads, both on guard duties as well as testing. Every single vehicle and weapon on base was being serviced, checked and tested. Patrols on foot continued throughout the day in full armour.

In all his time as a marine, Taylor had never seen the base so alive and determined. Everyone had been briefed on the retreat from the Moon and the potential threat which faced all of them. All serving officers and enlisted men and women were called to the base. Their families had been moved onto the base, under the protection of the Corps.

He looked up into the beautiful blue sky. A light breeze blew as the sun warmed his camouflaged BDUs. It was the perfect day to be sitting on a beach or going for a swim. It was hard to imagine that they were facing a major disaster the very next day. Mitch looked to the General's driver giving him a wave to say he would be not needed. A stroll back to his company quarters under the morning sun would be a welcome luxury while it was still possible.

Arriving back at the parade ground the Major found Suarez stood in front of eighteen marines who he didn't recognise. He had a Mappad in his hands and was checking through a list. The Lieutenant looked up to see Taylor approaching and quickly called the men to attention and saluted his commander.

"Stand easy!" shouted Taylor.

"Major, these are replacements for the company."

"So quickly? They must want us on the front line. New recruits?"

"No, Sir, transfers from other units, they have all served at least two years."

The Major looked up at the Lieutenant in surprise. There was never a time when they would be sent so many experienced men at once. The top brass must consider his company as essential to future operations.

"Any volunteers?"

"Yes, Sir, all of them."

Taylor turned to look at the men and women before him. From their posture each of them were confident and experienced marines. He moved along the line, carefully studying these new marines under his command. He stopped in front of an African-American woman who was as tall and broad shouldered as he was. Her eyes stayed ahead, her body unflinching under his gaze.

"Name?"

"Foster, Sir!"

"Well, Foster, you requested transfer to my unit, why?"

"Because I heard you were the best, Sir!"

He stepped back and paced up and down the line, finally turning back to the confident new men and women before him.

"Yesterday fourteen of this company were killed, nineteen wounded, four of which will never return to active service. As the only soldiers to have survived combat with this new enemy, the top brass sees us as a vital fighting force in what is likely going to be the largest war the world has ever known!"

He paced along the line, not a single marine commented or turned to face him, they were well disciplined.

"As part of this company you are guaranteed to see action, guaranteed the chance to die for your country.

None of us get paid enough for this work, so let me ask you all, are you willing to give everything you have to give to the Corps?"

"Sir, yes, Sir!" they shouted.

"Tomorrow you could follow me into a war the likes you never imagined, I expect the very best from each and every marine in this company. We look after our own. Welcome to D Company!"

There was a solemn silence following his introduction. They were experienced marines, although not experienced combat troops. They knew they were replacing fallen soldiers, but it was a grim reality of war to be reminded of it.

The day continued as a laborious and exhausting wait. There was nothing they could do to plan other than to clean and maintain their equipment. Taylor tried to convince the stores to equip his company with a greater range of heavy weapons, but to no avail. The warehouses were near empty, having every unit equipped for combat. Gear was already spread thin. Taylor was quickly coming to realise that his company were already better equipped than any, having been given special privileges due to their service.

The night was a lonely and uncomfortable one. Parker was on guard for most of it. He knew she'd be thinking of him as she patrolled the base. He acted as if there was nothing serious between them, as she did, but they both knew it was more than just a casual thing. Despite hating seeing his marines be killed and wounded, he was still thankful to have his closest and most trusted friends beside him.

Finally the Major fell into an uneasy sleep in the middle of the night, only to be awoken by the base sirens just as the sun was rising. He leapt out of his bed, ready for anything. Sweat clung to him and his vest was clammy, but there was nothing to be done about it. Pulling on his BDUs the Major was out of the building within three minutes of being awoken, with his pistol at his side.

Stepping through the doors of the officers' quarters he was confronted by the chaos of men rushing for their assembly points, the entire base had leapt into action. He looked up into the sky, but there was nothing of note. The sun was just piercing through the trees in the distance, beyond their vehicle training fields. There appeared to be no immediate threat. Before he could take a pace forwards the loudhailers fixed to every building rang out.

"All senior officers to the briefing centre!"

The command repeated a second time, but Taylor was already in full stride. Fifteen minutes later he sat among more than a hundred officers. The General was already waiting to brief them as they arrived. Normally there would be a deafening clatter of conversation, but not this time. The entire room was quiet as the last few officers shuffled into the room.

" Good morning, gentleman!" shouted General White.

The room was absolutely fixated on the General, knowing that it was time for serious news. Taylor felt his stomach turn, knowing that it would be exactly the kind of news he was hoping he wouldn't have to hear.

"The vast vessel which has been approaching us is now just out of Earth's orbit. It has however, not stopped. All sensors suggest that this country-sized ship is going to break into our atmosphere within the next hour, which we have now designated UFO1."

He sighed and looked around the room as everyone stared at him.

"As of this time, we still have no idea of the enemy's tactics or intentions. However, what we have seen so far would suggest a hostile intent. This unknown force is technologically advanced and highly capable, we need to avoid war if at all possible. For now we focus on defensive measures only. I want all ground troops ready to move at a moment's notice. Air cover will be in effect at all times for the foreseeable future."

The General looked down at the datapad in his hands. It was clear that he was surveying what little information he had and feeling helpless to act.

"For now we can do nothing but wait and watch. We are as ready as we can be. ROE are to not fire unless fired upon. Let's not start a war over a misunderstanding. That'll be all!"

The officers shuffled out of the room in remarkable silence. Nobody had anything left to say. Many were left speechless at the very idea of an alien invasion, others were letting their imaginations run wild with the possibilities.

* * *

Forty-five minutes had passed and Taylor's company had been posted half a mile outside the perimeter of the base. They had parked up the three trucks and two jeeps they'd been able to wrangle from the motor pool. It was a tight fit for the entire company to be carried in just five vehicles, with marines hanging off the sides as they drove. However, they were lucky, many units were entirely on foot, patrolling in the soaring heat.

The Major had ordered them to a halt a few moments before on the top of a small ridge overlooking the base and a small town in the distance the other side. He was sat on the bonnet of one of the jeeps, looking up at the sky and waiting to see the dreaded vessel. The piercing rays of the sun were putting him to sleep, until the radio of the vehicle rang out.

"Base to all units, UFO1 will be entering the atmosphere in approximately one minute!"

Taylor shrugged off his sleepiness and slipped off the vehicle's bonnet onto his feet. None of his men said a word. Most had already witnessed the savage and ugly enemy, but they were still intrigued to see the vast phenomenon.

The company could only watch in awe as the vast vessel burst through the clouds to the west. It must have been hundreds or even thousands of miles away, but was clear for everyone to see. The ship was a dark charcoal, almost black. It did not have the smooth lines that a human vessel would use for entering the atmosphere, but the harsh outline of a city's silhouette. They could make out little detail from the distance, except its vast engines. It was continuing east and well away from their base, a stark relief for all.

Taylor heard chatter coming from the vehicle, he walked back to his jeep to see that Suarez had got the news channel feeds on its display screen. He watched silently as cameras from all over the eastern seaboard tracking the behemoth as it soared easterly towards the Atlantic. The marines circled around the vehicle, as many of them as possible watching the screen, the rest listening quietly to the news anchor's dialogue.

The news channel was electric in its excitement over the situation. The idea of extraterrestrial life was a dream come true for reporters. The marines of D Company knew better, in that nothing good would come of a hostile force landing on Earth.

Taylor and the rest of his unit were fixated on the screen. An hour had passed as they watched the continued video feeds. The press kept repeating the same things, not having any real information to give beyond the actual footage of the immense craft. It was covering ground at an immense speed and heading right across the Atlantic. It was not long before the news agencies lost all trace of it and went back to repeating the footage they had.

As the team watched open mouthed, the radio cut in and Taylor was suddenly brought back to reality. He was being called back to base, while his men were ordered to continue a sweep of the area for the next two hours before returning to base.

"What do you think they want you for, Major?" Silva asked.

"Probably to ask me yet more questions that I cannot answer. Price, Kwori, you're with me. The rest of you, I know there doesn't appear to be an immediate threat, but we don't yet truly understand what we are dealing with. From now on you act as if under wartime conditions, be very vigilant!"

He jumped into the driver's seat as the other two men climbed aboard. He knew that he could no longer go anywhere alone. Not only could he not risk it as a company commander, but he was more than a little fearful of what could happen if he did. His experience on the Moon had shown that they needed substantial firepower to take down one of the heavily armoured enemy, but at least three guns were better than one.

⋆ ✳ ✳

Major Taylor found himself in yet another meeting of high-ranking officers. However, this time was different. They had some information to discuss, rather than just grilling him about the same matters again and again. The General had a map of the world up on the large screen at the end of the briefing table.

"It appears that UFO1 has come to a halt in the mid Atlantic. Unconfirmed reports are coming in that it has landed on the surface of the ocean. Now, let's just consider what this means. To call this a ship is a joke. Aerial shots have shown that since stopping, the vessel is expanding outwards. They have just created an eighth continent on our planet," said White.

"Has anyone made any attempt at contact?" asked General Smith.

"Communications in every way have been sent to the vessel. Every government has ordered its military to show no signs of hostility. So far we have heard no reports of any successful contact."

"General, this is a prelim to invasion, it's just a larger scale version of what we saw on the Moon," said Taylor.

"I am well aware of that, Major. But at his stage military action is not our decision to make. We follow the chain of command just as you do."

"Sir, the more time we give them to get established, the harder a time we are gonna have at holding them back. We should be preparing for full-scale war. We need to be equipping our troops with heavier guns and getting air strikes organised, nuclear if necessary!"

"Major! That's enough. I do not disagree with your assessment, but until we are given orders to do so, we will maintain our current alert level and be ready to respond to whatever orders are received."

A Lieutenant walked into the room and quickly went up to the General, passing him a datapad. The General studied it then looked up.

"The USS Doyle is just a few miles out from the landing zone of UFO1 and is attempting to make contact as we speak. We have video feeds from the deck."

The General pressed a few buttons and the map in front of him turned to a live feed from the bridge of the frigate. They could not contact the crew as they were in direct communication with the Pentagon, but they could see everything that the Navy crew could see. They gasped at the sheer vastness of what was there. The enemy vessel dominated the view ahead of them. Several parts of the ship were moving and expanding. It held still in the water like a landmass. The tall metal-like superstructure was a hundred metres above the surface. To those watching, it appeared as if a huge iron wall had just divided the Atlantic in half.

The entire room watched in awe and fear. For five whole minutes they watched the muted feed, seeing nothing more than the vast artificial island and occasionally the crew of the Doyle shuffling about.

"What the hell is that?" asked General White.

The officers squinted to look at small objects above UFO1.

"Fighter craft, the Doyle needs to engage its air defences immediately!" shouted Taylor.

"We cannot risk war!" Smith shouted.

"We are already at war, General!"

They turned back to the monitor just in time to see the two craft approaching and then light erupt from them. Seconds later the video feed cut off. They had no means to contact the Doyle to check its status, but they already knew what the answer would be. General White turned back to the table of officers with a grim expression on his face.

"It has begun, the Battle for Earth."

CHAPTER FIVE

Commander Kelly stepped back through the bunker doors where Colonel Visser was still hiding with his few guards. They'd managed to regain contact with some of the major buildings on the Moon colony through hard lines and were now able to watch the destruction on the security feeds. Kelly's head was cut and bleeding and sweat dripped from his face.

"Colonel! What the hell are you doing?" he shouted.

"The, the, people, we're lost!"

"Get your fucking head on your shoulders! I will not let these alien bastards take our homes without a fight!"

"Commander, we are finished here!"

Kelly slapped the UEN Colonel with the backhand of his glove, the hard platting striking his cheek and cutting the flesh.

"You were stationed here for a reason, Colonel! We are

soldiers, now act like one!"

The Colonel looked up at the video screens. The great metal clad monsters still stomped through the colony with their energy weapons blazing. The soldiers of the UEN and MDF were putting up a valiant fight but were being driven back in most sectors.

"What can we do? What can we do against such monsters?" cried Visser.

"We do whatever we have to do, Colonel! We are fighting for our very homes and lives!"

"I am sorry, Commander, but I have no choice but to surrender. I will not sit by and watch our people butchered. They are killing civilians and soldiers alike."

"You do whatever you have to do, Colonel, but my men will never lay down our arms!"

He stormed out of the room with eight of the MDF soldiers at his side. The cowardice of the UEN Colonel almost brought him to tears.

"Get a message out to all forces, amass around this building, we make our stand here!"

Kelly turned back, he had utter disdain for the Colonel and he would not let him surrender from the Prime Minister's own bunker. Let alone the fact that it was the strongest defensive location they had to hand. He rushed back into the room where Visser sat with his head in his hands. The Commander shook the man by his shoulders until he looked up at him.

"Colonel Visser, I am assuming command of all UEN forces on the colony, as you are unfit to command. You may surrender to the enemy, but you will do it alone, and not from this building. Now get out of my sight!"

* * *

"Hey, Charlie, what's the situation there?" asked Taylor.

The Major had just made contact with the British officer via live video feed. The Captain was in full armour with his rifle slung over his body.

"It's chaos here, I'm at the base in Rennes, France. We have lost contact with two EUA ships in the Atlantic. Everyone here is preparing for war, but officially we are still just on a high alert level, how is it there?"

"Same shit here. Everybody knows we're in for a fight but the bloody politicians are still pussy footing about. Keep in touch, Captain, we're going to need everything we've got over the coming days and weeks."

"Will do, good luck, Major."

The intercom cut off and Captain Jones turned and quickly strolled out of the field office into the open air of the Rennes base. The area was electric, alive like it had never been before. Armoured vehicles rolled around and aircraft flew overhead. The loudspeakers rang out and the huge viewing screens beside them fired into life. Brigadier Dupont addressed the base, something that had never happened before during his posting to Rennes.

"Attention all base personnel. As of 1500 hours, the unidentified vessel has landed in the Atlantic and appears to have expanded and established itself into a self-contained continent. We have lost contact with a number of naval vessels and there are reports of them being destroyed. Our scanners are at present showing that smaller vessels are approaching the French and Spanish coast lines in substantial numbers, with further airborne vehicles incoming."

The Brigadier took a deep breath as he sighed in disbelief about what he was having to read.

"At this stage, we must assume that we are in a state of war. You will shortly be receiving your orders through the chain of command. Two divisions from Rennes are being dispatched to the coast in preparation of any necessary defence. For those men and women who are being sent to defend our shores, know that you have the support of the world behind you. Good luck to you all, and Godspeed!"

The video feeds cut out and announcements rang out across the base for all personnel to report immediately to their base commanders and designated rally points. Lieutenant Green and Corporal Hughes stepped up beside Jones as he made his way to his battalion formation area.

"Think we'll be heading to the front line, Sir?" asked Hughes.

"Almost certainly, there are only three full divisions

combat ready on the base and they'll want to keep one of the French divisions here for the defence of the city."

"You think they're concerned that we wouldn't be able to hold them back?"

"Yes, Green. We're facing an unknown enemy with unknown capabilities. They'd be fools to send everything to the front line, a system of layered defence has proven advantageous on countless occasions during invasion."

Minutes later Jones arrived at the Battalion Divisional officers' meeting while the rest of the men assembled on the parade grounds, eagerly awaiting news of who would be sent to face this new threat.

"Gentlemen, time is of the essence here, so I will be brief. Your division, along with the 2nd Armoured French Division, is being dispatched immediately to the west coast. As of this time we have absolutely no idea of the enemy strength or intentions. The two divisions will be tasked with the defence of the coast from Brest to Nantes. It's a lot of ground to cover, but the reality is we are against the clock here. Enemy forces will be at the coastline in a matter of hours. Any questions you have will have to be answered via communication en route. That'll be all, gentlemen, good luck," said Dupont.

The officers all turned and rushed out of the room. They were beginning to understand the severity of the situation. They knew the military capability of units in the area, and knew that it could be days before further units could be deployed in any capacity.

Reaching his platoon, the men were already fully formed up beside their vehicles. As an infantry unit in peacetime deployment they were only equipped with unarmoured vehicles, but that would at least allow them to cover ground quickly. He surveyed his men, they carried no field equipment, only ammunition and body armour. A hasty deployment would get them in action quickly, but they'd need re-supplying fast.

"Mount up!" Jones ordered.

The parachute regiment platoon consisted of three sections of ten men, as well as a four-man command section, which included Lieutenant Green, himself and his batman, Private Saunders. The platoon loaded up into two open top trucks while the command section took the Captain's personal vehicle, a Rapid Deployment Vehicle (RDV). In the vein of the WW2 Jeep, the RDV was a lightweight, open top all terrain vehicle. It was capable of carrying four personnel and had a passenger mounted BRUN light machinegun.

It was a hundred kilometres to the coastline and travelling in convoy their speed would be reduced. Typically their battalion would be deployed using aircraft, which would have sped up their deployment. But all aircraft in Rennes were being used to transport the armoured divisions' vehicles, or to collect and deploy troops to the border of the city.

Getting to the coastline was not at all a concern for Jones. It would be a ninety-minute drive to reach the very start of the positions they had to defend. What concerned him more was that without a good supply of aircraft they'd have no fast way back. He'd heard from Major Taylor about the combat ability of the enemy they faced, and it was more than eye opening. He was only thankful that they could fight on home soil back on Earth.

* * *

The convoy was on the outskirts of Brest. Captain Jones had been briefed, but being only a platoon leader he knew that he'd only been given half the story. His communication with Major Taylor had put him in a better stead than most of the units, but he still felt more than just uneasy.

"Hey, Sir, why aren't the population evacuating?" asked Saunders.

The officer's batman was driving the RDV and Jones sat in the commander's seat at the machine gun.

"At this stage we simply do not know what to expect, Private. Evacuating a major city would create chaos and need immense resources. More importantly, from our perspective the roads would be clogged as panic rapidly spread. Right now the priority is that we get troops at the coast as a barrier to whatever threat exists, if any."

"So we just leave the people here and hope they'll be

ok?"

The Captain sighed as he looked out across the old city and imagined the huge innocent civilian population that inhabited it. He didn't like it either, but he had his orders.

"Think of it this way. Private. If whatever is coming up those beaches cannot be stopped by two divisions, then what good would such a late evacuation do?"

The Private went silent. The very idea that so many thousands of the finest troops in the world could be cast aside was a chilling thought to dwell upon. The radio cut in and it ordered the parachute battalion to head for a beach south of the city. The 2nd Parachute Battalion was attached to a regular British infantry division.

Jones looked at his Mappad, it showed the positions all the units had taken up. The two divisions we spread across a fifteen-kilometre line of the coast. Most of the armour was around the traditional old naval city, though some of the heavier equipment could not be airlifted and was still en route via road.

Having no armour support was a daunting thought to the men of the parachute regiment. Jones knew how heavily armoured their enemy was and the fearful circumstances the airborne forces were now facing.

They eventually rolled up at the desolate beach. It was a mix of stone and sand. It would be a pleasant place to spend time on a warm day, though many of the men were already familiar with it, having spent time there. The barren area provided little cover beyond small embankments and dunes.

As the battalion took up its position across the beachhead they were struck by the intimidating sight of the enemy ships approaching. They could only make out a rough blurred shape of each as they used the same chameleon camouflage technology Taylor had described. However, the spray gave their position away. They were all thankful for radar and other sensory technology, otherwise the coast would have gone undefended.

Captain Jones stood up on a grass embankment and held up his binoculars to his eyes. The enemy vessels could be seen as far as he could see either side of their position. The binoculars were having difficulty calculating the size of the near invisible craft. Six were heading for the area they were covering. Jones turned pack to his platoon, some were lying prone against the mounds, others standing open mouthed. All were watching the approaching forces.

"Right, boys! No time to dig in, get the BRUNs ready and take up positions!"

Within two minutes the entire platoon lay silently beyond the raised earth and dunes, looking over the bleak coastline. They were less than two hundred metres from the water, perfect range to lay down fire. The intercoms of each man in the unit cut in, Brigadier Dupont was addressing all men of both divisions as one.

"This is Dupont. Anticipate a hostile enemy, but do not

fire unless fired upon. Remember, if it comes to it, they are weaker at their joints and face. Good luck to you all!"

Jones knew that the Brigadier would be surveying the situation from long distance, likely still in the Rennes base, though he didn't envy him. The Captain had signed up for the kind of adventure and wars that he'd read about and witnessed on the news as a child, not the uncertainty of an advanced alien race. The unknown was scarier to the men than any army in the world.

"You heard the Brigadier, not a single shot unless we are fired upon!" shouted Jones.

He stared at the mysterious and imposing craft. They were travelling at a vast speed across the water. He wondered for a moment at their intentions. With no communication, it appeared odd to him that they would simply attack. As far as he was aware, no human had shown any aggression towards whoever they were. As they were just a few hundred metres from the shoreline the vehicles slowed and their cloaking technology came off.

They appeared crude in design, with harsh lines. Earth ships had long been designed to be incredibly efficient, whether they travelled by air or water. These craft appeared to use immense power with little finesse. The skins were of a raw metal-like fabric, and they were almost twice the size of a main battle tank. Jones shot a glance around at his men.

"Have we got the ARMAL launchers with us?"

"Yes, Sir, but for what?" Hughes asked.

"Just get them ready!"

They had three of the anti-armour launchers in their platoon, one for each section. The devices folded up onto the backs of the men carrying them. At ranges of up to a hundred metres they were capable of taking out light to medium armoured vehicles, and even something heavier at close range if it hit the sweet spot.

The time for preparation was over. The platoon watched in horror as the vehicles slid up onto the beaches, but they didn't stop. Tracks on either side running the length and outline of the vehicles began to spin, pulling the huge craft onto the beach. The giant metal monsters resembled enlarged versions of WW1 tanks, which they had only ever seen in movies and museums.

"Jesus Christ!" shouted Saunders.

"Keep it down!"

The tracked monsters were crawling up the beach at less than ten kilometres an hour. Jones hoped that was all they were capable of, but he knew that they would not have such luck. Hatches at the rear of the vehicles struck the beach as they continued, and then they saw them, just as Taylor's report had said. The massive creatures stepped out as the tanks continued forward.

"We're gonna need air support," said Green.

"Remember, no contact unless we are engaged," Jones ordered.

"You think these bastards have come for a picnic?"

"Command will be seeing what's going on, they'll do whatever they deem necessary."

"Yeah, while we get our balls blown off!"

Jones turned back to the incoming alien forces and watched as the last of the steel monsters clambered out of the vehicles. They were not graceful creatures, but he could only watch in awe at their striking image. Eight of the armoured soldiers exited from each of the six vehicles. Forty-eight against the battalion's almost seven hundred men were the sort of odds that any soldier would like, but not here.

The vehicles suddenly came to a close and the massive soldiers spread out between them. It was if they had stopped to admire the view, looking around in every direction. To Jones they were the aliens, but he realised to them, everything on Earth was alien. As the soldiers stepped from the hard wet sand of the waterline, they began to sink into the sand.

For a moment the Captain thought the enemy had underestimated the terrain, and a few of his lads began to laugh. Seconds later, the armoured soldiers pressed buttons on their suits and giant webbed feet extended from their spring legs, giving the same effect as snow shoes, expanding their surface area. The men of the platoon laughed no longer, they were quickly learning that this was not an enemy to be taken lightly.

"What do we do, Sir?"

"Absolutely nothing, Green, this is their move."

The enemy surveyed the line of mounds and dunes where the battalion was set up. It was fairly clear that they had spotted the troops, what was uncertain was their intentions. Guns began to rise from the roof sections of the tanks, but they were comparatively small for the size of vehicles. As the guns locked into position the vehicles started to roll forward, the soldiers between them. Then without warning, light erupted from their weapons.

Huge pulses of light landed around their positions, they could feel the heat from each blast even ten metres away. For whatever technology they did have, targeting equipment did not seem to be their strong point.

"What do we do, Sir?" screamed Saunders.

"Hold!"

An explosion ripped down the line of defences in the platoon next to theirs. One of the rounds hit a man square on and blew his body apart, cauterising the bloody wounds in the process from the immense heat. Smoke arose from the body as one of his comrades screamed in pain from a lesser injury.

"Fire!" shouted Jones.

The beachhead erupted into a constant bellowing of gunfire. The accurate shooting of the para boys would have flattened a human wave attack, but the metal monsters continued forwards. The cannon-like turret mounted weapons on the vehicles fired in a slow but almost continuous barrage. Two of Jones' platoon were hit by rounds from enemy fire. Over the gunfire he could already hear the screams for help and the cries of pain, he could do nothing about it, they needed every gun firing.

One of the alien soldiers stepped ahead of the rest and he was immediately targeted by half the battalion's gunfire. The amount of metal smashing into his armour forced the creature to a standstill, until finally it collapsed through injuries sustained.

"That's it, boys, take them down!"

The enemy tanks began to gain pace and were now within just a hundred metres of them. Jones turned to see his company commander running down the lines. Three of his platoon were dead and two more wounded.

"Get the ARMALs into action!"

They all had radio comms, but Jones knew many of the men would be too distracted by the fire fight and their fallen comrades to listen to any commands given. One of the men a few metres to his side lifted the device onto his shoulder and took aim. Before he could fire he was hit by one of the enemy weapons, taking half his face off and rendering the weapon useless.

Jones dropped back gasping at the slaughter around him. He turned to the other two men who lay against the embankment with the launchers.

"Get up there and fire!"

The Captain pulled himself up to survey the situation and lifted his rifle into view. Four of the creatures lay dead or at least incapacitated on the sand, but it was a small relief compared to the casualties of the battalion.

The first ARMAL fired, a large smoke plume erupting from the launcher. The rocket soared towards the first vehicle at high speed and smashed into it. The round ignited into a huge flash as it struck. The vehicle continued on through the smoke cloud, its armour scorched and torn. The men could see that they had damaged it, just not enough.

Looking down the line of paras, Jones could already see that the other platoons were putting their launchers into effect. Seconds later three launchers fired almost in sequence at the same vehicle. The second caused it to burst into flames and draw to a halt. The third padded through the gaping hole in the armour and must have finished off whatever was controlling the vehicle, as no one made an attempt to escape.

Cries of victory and excitement rang out across the line of defences as the men threw their arms up in the air and shouted abuse at their attackers. The enemy didn't seem fazed by the destruction of their vehicle and continued on towards the soldiers.

"Alright, reload and give them all you've got!" shouted Jones.

Major Stewart, Jones' company commander, ran up to

their position and threw himself onto the embankment beside the Captain. His ear was bleeding and his radio earpiece was hanging loose.

"Are you okay, Sir?"

"The Colonel is dead, Captain, HQ staff with him!"

The Major was shouting, his hearing was blown and he was still in a state of shock, perhaps disorientated as well.

Jones looked quickly back over the defences and fired three bursts at the nearest attacker. Smoke trails let out from along the lines as every platoon tried to take out the enemy tanks with their ARMAL launchers. He looked back to the stricken Major.

"Who's in charge of the battalion, Sir?"

"I am, Captain! What do I do?"

Jones looked down at the Major, his hands were empty. He reached across to one of the bodies of his fallen men and tugged the rifle from the dead soldier's hands. He thrust it into the clutches of the Major.

"Get up there and start shooting!"

The Captain returned the same target he'd been firing at, the armoured beast was now staggering, its leg armour damaged. He let out several well-aimed bursts at the mirrored section of what he thought was its face, just as Taylor had advised. A gunner beside him targeted the same spot with sustained fire from his BRUN gun, the glass-like section shattered sending the Mech stumbling into the sand in a crumpled and twisted mess.

A pulse of light flashed past Jones' head. He ducked but was fortunate that it was already off target, the heat of the shot singed his face and eyebrows. He turned to see Saunders cradling his arm to his side. His batman was wounded and his armour and clothing were smouldering. He had no sympathy for the man, not when their friends were dying around them.

"Saunders! Get your arse up there and keep fighting!"

He crawled up to the top of the embankment to see the carnage of the battlefield. At least fifteen of the Mechs were now destroyed, but he could see dead and wounded men all along their defences. The enemy were just thirty metres from their position and still approaching at a steady pace.

"Grenades!" he shouted.

Every man in the battalion carried two grenades. The high explosive fragmentation grenades had a blast radius of five metres and were highly effective against the regular infantry armours that Earth forces used. Jones drew out his first grenade and twisted the firing mechanism, looking around to see others doing the same before quickly throwing it as far as he could. Ducking back behind cover, he waited and hoped.

Explosions ignited all along the line of the attackers. Seconds later they were joined by bellowing shells from the north, far louder than anything on their battlefield. Jones turned to look to the north, but the land obscured his view. Over and over they heard cannons firing.

"It's the 2nd Armoured!" shouted Green.

The men wanted to cheer, but they were too distracted by the enemy closing in on them.

"Alright, boys, give them everything you've got!" Jones ordered.

He twisted the trigger on his second grenade and threw it over the top, immediately lifting his rifle and opening fire. The battalion brought its full weight to bare, grenades, ARMAL launchers and machine guns. Despite the hailstorm of bullets and rockets, the Mechs continued to fire. Explosions erupted all across the sands as the tanks were punctured and set on fire, the armoured soldiers crippled and destroyed.

Finally, the beach went silent, only the heavy guns to the north continued to roar. Captain Jones stood up on the embankment and looked down the length of the defences. He could see medics working desperately to patch up and save the wounded. There were six dead in his platoon alone and several wounded.

"Saunders, get onto the Brigadier, inform him that we have held the beachhead but sustained heavy casualties!"

He looked out to the burning wrecks of the vehicles and the collapsed armoured soldiers around them.

"The rest of the platoon with me!"

Jones released the magazine from his rifle, slipping in a new clip as he walked cautiously. He lifted his rifle to his shoulder and kept it ready to fire at a moment's notice. Black smoke bellowed from the flames of the vehicles, but they were fortunate that the winds blew it south.

"Shoot anything that moves!"

He carefully walked up to the first Mech's body. It was on its back with one of its legs buckled from an explosion, likely from a grenade. Staring at the armour more closely, it was not as crude as first thought. The design work was brutish and harsh, but the quality of construction was fine engineering.

Kneeling down beside the body, he rested his hand on the metal work. It was smooth, as if highly polished, yet the finish was quite dull. He tapped it with the plated knuckles of his gloves. It was thick, he guessed about ten millimetres. He lifted one of the lifeless arms of the suit and it was surprisingly light. He could only imagine that the metal was of an unknown material.

The Major turned back to look at the positions they had fought from. There were craters all along the embankments and scattered bodies. His curiosity about the enemy was over, all he cared about was that they were dead. He moved back to the defences as gunshots rang out behind him. The last few living Mechs were being finished off with no mercy.

He stopped next to an army medical corps officer who was attending a wounded man. The enemy's energy weapon had burnt through the flank of the chest section, taking some of the man's flesh with it. Major Stewart sat near them with his head in his hands.

"Major, what are the total casualties?"

The officer said nothing, not even turning to look at the Captain.

"Major!"

The doctor turned and answered the question himself, understanding the state of shock Stewart was experiencing.

"Reports so far for the battalion are ninety-five dead, thirty-six wounded. These weapons don't leave many casualties."

Jones shook his head. Their unit had never lost more than three soldiers on any operation in the last ten years. The officers in charge of the other companies strolled into view, their faces were wrought with despair. They were led by Major Chandra, a bold woman, and the only female to lead a company in the parachute regiment.

"Captain, The Colonel is dead, we've also lost quite a few other officers and NCOs."

"Major Stewart is unfit for command and I have relieved him, with his permission."

Chandra nodded, it was the worst day of her illustrious career. Never could she have imagined so much carnage among such a fine troop of soldiers.

"You are now commanding D Company?" she asked.

"Yes, Sir."

"Then I am making you Acting Commander of D

Company. I am the senior officer left here and am assuming command of the Battalion."

"Yes, Sir."

"We've faced a shit storm here, Captain, but we cannot afford to slack and lick our wounds. Assign a replacement to command your platoon, have your troops salvage any ammunition from the dead and start digging in."

"Sir!"

"What the hell is that?" shouted Green.

Captain Jones turned to look out into the Atlantic. He was squinting to make out what was behind the trailing black smoke plumes from the wrecked vehicles. He raised his binoculars not believing what he could see. On the horizon he could make out the same blurred outlines of the enemy amphibious tanks steaming towards the shoreline. They were just thirty minutes out at the most, and in greater numbers.

"My, God!"

* * *

"Keep firing!" shouted Kelly.

The MDF men stood in three lines firing repeatedly at the metal monsters as they went around the corner of the narrow corridor up ahead. Two of the Mechs were already down. In the close range they could concentrate their fire well against single enemies, although they had little cover. Their comrades lay strewn among the dead civilians in every area of the colony. The third armoured soldier before them dropped lifeless to the deck.

"Sir, we must fall back!" shouted Private Lewis.

Kelly looked around the corridor at the carnage. A number of his comrades were wounded, many more were dead or dying in the ground they had already fought over. They had put up a noble fight and had brought down many a foe, but he knew they were fighting a losing battle.

"I will not give up our homeland!"

"Sir, we've already lost it, all that's left are the people!"

The Commander looked around in despair, a small trickle of blood dripped down his worn and tired face where the impact from an explosion had knocked him against an interior wall. His face was black with dirt and sweat, he ached in every bone and muscle in his body. He was almost brought to tears, knowing that they had lost everything they'd fought for.

Commander Kelly had been in charge of the Moon Defence Force for twenty-two years, a role that he had inherited from his father. Never could he have imagined that he would have to concede it to a technologically advanced alien race, which appeared to want nothing more but to execute them all.

"Alright, fall back to the bunker!"

The Private looked relieved as he sent out the command to their forces. However, it didn't completely remove the worry from his face. No one knew if surrender was even a possibility against the iron army they fought. The Commander turned and led his men back to the re-enforced blast bunker.

As he approached the lines of dead and dying lining the corridors confronted him. Anyone still able to hold a gun was stood or propped up outside the blast doors. The men did their best to stand to attention as the Commander went past them, but many were gritting their teeth under the pain of their injuries. Kelly smiled back at them in appreciation, desperately trying to hide his sorrow.

He went straight up to the comms officer who was watching the video feeds that were still operational. He rubbed his eyes and squinted to make out what he was seeing from the rooftop cameras.

"It's Colonel Visser, Sir."

Kelly studied the video intently. The Colonel was standing on the roof of the government building in his compression suit. He wore no weapons and only held one object, a white flag slung on an l-shape pole.

"What the hell is he doing? He's surrendering, or trying to!"

"Maybe we should join him," said Lewis.

Before Kelly could respond he watched as a glimmer panned across the screen, an enemy vessel in its terrain mapping camouflage. The vessel landed on the rooftop just thirty metres from the Colonel. He still held the white flag high in both arms. The Commander hated Visser for being a coward earlier on in the fight, but now he hoped with all his heart that he would come to no harm.

The vessel's chameleon device switched off as a door opened and three armoured aliens stomped out onto the roof. Visser stood his ground. They could see that he was trying to speak to them, under the hope that they might understand something of what he said, or at least his intentions.

Of the three armoured soldiers, the one at the front stood out from the rest. The armour was decorated with a golden coloured banding on the corner edges and painted with symbols that meant nothing to them. This creature held some form of authority over the rest.

"What are they doing, Sir?" asked Lewis.

"I don't know."

As the men watched the screens in both anticipation and fear, the lead alien lifted his arm and fired a small pulse weapon attached to his arm. The shot blasted straight through Colonel Visser's chest and out the back, leaving a gaping hole. He died instantly. None of them said a word.

In that moment Kelly knew that their struggle was far from over. There was no surrender, no retreat. He turned to his men, thirty soldiers surrounded the desks, many more were waiting outside the bunker. He had a grim expression on his face. Gone was the warmness in his heart, replaced with shear hatred, all he had left was survival and revenge.

"There it is for you all to see! These bastards don't just want our land. They want our lives! You have only two choices before you, lay down and die, or fight!"

The room remained silent as they all clung to his words. Many of their families were already dead and many more were unaccounted for. At fifty-eight years of age, Kelly never expected that he would ever have to lead a serious combat operation, let alone an army.

"This colony has endless underground corridors, bunkers and research tunnels. We can no longer hold onto ground, we can no longer fight in open war. Today we go underground. Tomorrow we fight back. Let no one be unclear here. The following days and weeks will be more horrific than any of you can imagine. Earth is at war and we have no rescue in sight. But I'll be damned if I am going to die without a fight! Who is with me?"

CHAPTER SIX

Major Taylor sat in his chair beside the senior officers on base. General White had just outlined the current situation. Spain and France had been invaded. Spain had taken the brunt of the attack, France had substantially more time to prepare and with a far greater number of operational EUA forces at hand. He had not heard news of Captain Jones, but he knew that he'd be on the front line.

"Spain has already lost fifty kilometres of its western coast. Early reports from France show that although the initial attacks were repulsed, they were at a dear price. The Americas have so far been lucky in avoiding invasion, but we cannot stay out of this conflict. The UEN forces are already involved in heavy fighting, we have a responsibility to act."

"What are the President's orders?" asked Smith.

"The President would avoid war at any cost as we well

know. However, this is not like any war this planet has ever known. Whoever these hostile forces are, it is clear that they only want two things, our lands and our lives," said White.

"We are at war, our friends around the world are dying as we talk, what are we prepared to do about it?" asked Taylor.

"I will remind you, Major, that you are here under an advisory capacity only," said General White.

"Fine, Sir, then I advise an immediate strike against the alien ship, island, whatever the damn thing is."

"Quite right, Major. The time has come to act. We have already lost men in this war. The President, under the advisement of the Chiefs of Staff, has passed on operational decisions to us, as well as given me control of the Nuclear arsenal," General White answered him.

General Smith turned in shock.

"Nuclear?"

"This new enemy is gaining a substantial foothold in Europe, they have shown themselves to be a formidable enemy which could engulf the world if we do nothing. I am not asking for a vote here, I am informing you of my decision. I am authorising an immediate nuclear strike against the alien island, now designated as Tartaros, a hell that no man would wish to see."

The General tapped a few buttons on his control pad and brought up a map of the world. The vast island had expanded to more than five hundred kilometres in diameter in the Atlantic. It was a shocking sight every time they had to look at it. The chilling image could only give a small taste of what it would be like to witness the horrifying development with one's own eyes.

"Six of our nuclear depots are prepping for launch as we speak. The initial attack will contain twelve missiles launched from these six bases."

"What are our projections for damage to this Tartaros?" asked General Richards.

"Honestly at this stage, we have no idea. We simply cannot sit by and watch these bastards continue unchecked. Our nuclear arsenal allows us to strike hard and fast, with maximum coverage. Obviously this Tartaros is now the size of many large countries. We have indicators of the best targets. This will be a test run. If it works, it will be immediately followed with everything we've got."

"And if it doesn't?"

"We have to try, gentlemen. If for some reason a nuclear strike has no significant impact, then we'll change tactics, improvise and overcome."

"What about ground troops?" asked Taylor.

"At this stage every soldier in the country is on alert and ready to fight. How we use our forces will depend on the outcome of this strike," White answered.

"What about Europe? It's taking a beating!" Richards asked him.

"I am told that forces are being drawn from all across the continent to fight in France and Spain, for now they'll have to manage. Now, launch is in five minutes, with impact approximately fifteen minutes after."

"Jesus Christ, are we really doing this?" asked Smith.

"You're damn right we are. People are dying every minute fighting against these bastards, it's time to give a little back!" shouted White.

The room went silent as they all sat watching the huge screen, captivated by the launch countdowns next to each nuclear depot. The idea of using nuclear weapons was fearful for all of them. There had only been a handful of cases where they had been used previously in Earth's history, and the results were always terrifying. The President called them a necessary evil but the few Generals who didn't support his view were starting to come around.

The next twenty minutes were almost silent, with the very least of communication. The high ranking officers shuffled in their chairs, drank water to clear their dry throats and continued to watch the screen as the trails of the missiles sped across the sea. None of them ever thought that they would see the use of such weapons in their lifetimes, let alone to be the ones launching them.

General White pressed a few buttons on his control pad and the huge screen split to show several video feeds of the enemy island. The top left of the monitor continued to project the map showing the progress of the missiles.

The group watched with baited breath, knowing that the President and the joint chiefs would be doing the same.

The nuclear weapon was still the most formidable weapon in the arsenal of Earth troops. With no major wars for so long, there had been few significant advancements made in weapons of war. Many believed no one wished to consider the development of a weapon that could destroy more than just a city. Other governments were unable to continue with such massive spending into weapons of mass destruction when they had plenty good enough ones already.

"What the hell is that?" asked Smith.

Taylor squinted to look at what they were seeing, realising quickly what it was. Dozens of aircraft were lifting off from one section of the enemy vessel, obscured by their scenery blending camouflage.

"Enemy ships, Sir, just as attacked the Moon colony," said Taylor.

"What are they doing, Major?" asked White.

"I'd assume they are intercepting our nukes."

White twisted around quickly and looked at the Major with a piercing glance.

"What? You think they intend to shoot our weapons down?"

"Of course, Sir. You think we are the only ones with scanners? Everything we have seen so far shows us that these aliens are significantly more advanced than us. What is maybe more of a concern is, if we have nukes, what have they got?"

The room went quiet again as they all stared intently at the screens. The missiles were just minutes away from impact. The officers could almost feel the sense of victory they so desperately wanted, but knew it was beyond their grasp. They'd all come to realise that the mission was already a failure, but they still held onto the hope that it would succeed.

The Generals watched in despair and horror as energy pulses were fired from the vessels, striking the nuclear missiles as they were fifty kilometres from the alien island. A number of the enemy craft were obliterated by the huge nuclear blasts, but it was a small loss for them. Many of the camera feeds went blank as the blasts destroyed the source of the signals.

General White shook his head, his face pale and distraught. The others watched the blank screens which displayed only static. The satellite signals showed Tartaros, it was unscathed by the incident.

"My, God," said Richards.

"We only sent twelve, maybe with a larger spread they wouldn't be able to catch them all?" asked Smith.

General White looked up, he was struggling to speak, and for the first time in his career, Taylor saw fear in the great leader's eyes.

"Let's see this for what it is. Those bastards have the

defensive technology to stop a missile strike. Let's move past it and see what we can do."

Taylor still stared at the display screen of the world, wondering what they could do against such an enemy. His gaze panned to Europe and he began to wonder if his friend Charlie was still alive.

* * *

"Fall back! Go, go, go!" shouted Jones.

Light pulses zipped past their heads as the metal clad beasts and their monstrous armoured vehicles rolled through the streets. The defences to the south of Brest had fallen into disarray as the invaders were punching huge holes in their line. The French armour still remained in the city but were fighting a brutal battle of attrition.

Captain Jones looked around to see the survivors of their battalion running for their lives, he could just make out the fearful outline of the Mech soldiers stomping towards them in the distance and firing unrelentingly into the fleeing troops. Major Chandra rushed up to Jones with blood hardened on her face, it wasn't clear if it was hers, but Jones was glad she was still in command.

"What are you orders, Major?" shouted Jones.

"We can't hold this area, get to the vehicles and mount up, we're heading for Brest! If we can rendezvous with the 2nd Armoured and make use of the cover of the city, we might just have a chance!"

Jones nodded and turned to relay the commands to his men. Every instinct made the Captain wish they were heading east towards the rest of their forces at Rennes. Despite this, he realised both the importance of protecting the civilian population and also of holding ground. If the invaders could get a hold on the mainland they would gain a major advantage.

None of the men wanted to accept the fact that they were at war, but it was the new reality of their lives. Jones sent the command out across the radios and they began to run for the vehicles. They left many dead soldiers in their wake, carrying all the wounded they could.

Arriving at the vehicles, Jones could see that half of his company was already loaded up, many were wounded, there were not many left to load up. At a quick glance he estimated the losses to be thirty percent of the company, with many others being walking wounded. He stood up on his RDV and looked back towards the beaches now out of view. Smoke still bellowed from the wrecks there. They were joined with a number of fires on trees and foliage that had ignited from the high heat energy pulses of the enemy.

"Get a fucking shift on!" he shouted.

The last men were being pulled aboard the trucks. He could see that the company was mentally exhausted. Their resolve and morale had taken a heavy blow and they were already moving like defeated men. Overcoming this would be Jones' next big task, but for now, survival was the only priority.

"Move out!"

His vehicle moved forward as his batman enthusiastically raced ahead. No one among them desired to stay in that spot for a second longer. As the battalion sped north towards the city, energy pulses were fired amongst the column. Jones watched as one of the trucks was hit, the engine bay and front axle obliterated as it flipped onto its side.

Jones wanted nothing more to go back and help the soldiers, but being in full retreat he couldn't risk slowing anyone else down. The Captain could see that Chandra had seen the incident and was already on the comms to the survivors, instructing them to make their way north through the cover of the forest. He prayed that they would make it but knew their chances were slim. Realising that their first battle was over, Jones slumped down in the seat of the RDV with a sigh. They were fighting such a fearful and advanced force.

Minutes later they were out of the range of the invaders and Jones turned his attention to their destination. Up ahead they could hear the thunderous echo of the tank guns of the French Armoured Division. Machine guns rattled off in the distance as the battle raged on. He could make out the continuous trail of civilian vehicles pouring out of the easterly flyover heading for Morlaix. All Jones could think was that it wasn't far enough.

Their column was rolling towards an absolute war zone, and the Captain knew exactly how on edge his troops were at that moment. They were one of the best trained fighting forces in the world, but the prospect of going from one defeat into a second battle in the same day was morale crushing. Sadly, he knew that there was no choice. Troops would be amassing in Rennes, but it would take time, for now, they were it.

Dust and smoke poured from locations across the old coastal city as they rolled into the urban outskirts. All around them were civilians desperately trying to load their vehicles and leave. Many asked for help, but the only help they could provide was to fight the invading enemy. The call came out on the radio for A and B Companies to halt at the southern inner city district and take up positions.

Jones' company followed on with Major Chandra to the city centre and the western district where the fighting raged on. The inner city was completely abandoned, few vehicles remained and no people in sight. People's possessions and businesses' stock were scattered across the roads. The population had run in fear of their lives, which was the sad reality of their situation. The convoy came to a halt and the Captain stepped out of the vehicle looking around the desolate city, before issuing his orders.

"Company dismount, take up defensive positions

around the convoy. Command section with me."

Lieutenant Green now commanded the Captain's platoon. Every man in their force was trained and instructed on how to fulfil the tasks of those above them, should the need ever arise. No one had ever expected such a responsibility to fall upon them. Jones continued forwards along the line of the convoy with the few men of his command section at his side.

Up ahead they could see a number of light armoured vehicles parked up at a crossroads. The French Lieutenant Colonel Girard, leader of the 2nd Armoured Division was looking at a map projection of the city that was set up on the bonnet of one of their scout vehicles. Beside him was Major Chandra. They were in a heated discussion, but Jones could not merely stand by and watch.

"Ah, Captain, step up please. Colonel Girard, this is Captain Jones, recently promoted to Company Commander."

"Captain. Let us get back to the battle. I brought a little under two hundred and fifty tanks to Brest. Now I command only one hundred and eighty. Our infantry battalions are having difficulty holding back the enemy, we cannot hold out for much longer."

"What do you suggest, Colonel?" Chandra asked.

"What is the situation of the rest of the British Division?"

"My battalion is at about sixty percent strength. The

armoured units we had have mostly been driven back or destroyed. We haven't got the heavy armour of your division. Many of the units have retreated to Landerneau, we are simply unable to hold the lines."

"Colonel, there are still a lot of civilians leaving the city via the main roads, we can neither travel on those routes, nor leave them to the mercy of our enemy," Jones added.

The French Colonel gasped as he looked down the length of the western street. Their main battle tanks could be seen fighting at the end of it.

"Then we fight on, as long as we can, we have no choice," said Girard.

Jones nodded in agreement. They knew that they were condemning many of their soldiers to death, but it was their duty to defend the citizens and lands with their lives.

"Have the troops you have in Landerneau set up on the main road to Morlaix and Rennes. They'll be needed as a barrier defence to the enemy and to defend our route back."

"You think they'll need to use our roads?" asked Chandra.

"From what we have seen so far, yes. They have aircraft, but if they are using sea and land craft to transport troops, then they'll need solid roads to cover distance quickly," said Jones.

"How long can we hold out here in Brest?"

"Your guess is good as mine, Major, we'll do what we

can. Have your battalion set up on the southern perimeter of the city centre as a defensive line against anything coming up from the beaches. If any more of your division roll in, send them to me. Good luck, Major."

Chandra nodded and saluted as she turned to leave. They both knew that they were being asked to set up against the very invading troops that had just driven them from the beaches, but at least this time they had the cover of the terrain, and the French armour at their backs.

"Where is the rest of the division, Major?" Jones asked her.

"Mostly as I told the Colonel. At least some of our troops got cut off down south and are retreating further inland, but they are mostly scattered to the wind. It appears we have about a brigade strength in Landerneau, driven back quickly from the positions north of the city, as well as just south of our original position."

"Sounds like it's chaos."

"It is, Captain, we've never had to deal with anything like this. Command structure is in tatters, many of the key officers of the division are dead or wounded. Brigadier Dupont appears completely out of touch with the situation on the ground. All that we know for certain is that we have at least a sizeable force in this city, and we will do our best to defend it."

"If we stay much longer, there'll be no way out for any of us!"

"I am aware of that, Captain. As the only known forces to still hold coastal ground, we are giving the EUA time to gather forces and for the civilians to evacuate east. These are our only priorities at this time."

"Yes, Sir."

"Oh, and another thing. The situation is strictly between us, I won't have the morale of our troops pulled down any further, understood?"

"Sir."

"Captain, we've got a job to do, go to it!"

Jones nodded and continued on towards his company. They were spread out in the street, taking cover near the buildings. He could see the worry in their faces and the lack of faith in their equipment. The prospect of an enemy so superior in firepower, armour and strength had never even been considered a possibility for the men of the division. He could see that one of the platoon trucks had been allocated as a med station for wounded only.

Of the one hundred and fifty men in his company, only two thirds were still standing. Many of those had suffered glancing hits or concussion from near misses. He was left with a physically and mentally crippled body of soldiers. He knew without a doubt that what they needed more than anything else was to get out of the hostile zone and re-group. None of them had ever seen serious combat, they needed time to recover and re-gain some confidence.

It was even clearer to Captain Jones that they needed

one thing more than anything else, bigger guns. They outnumbered the alien invaders in every fight, but didn't have the individual firepower to bring them down.

"Let's get this street closed down, I want dragon's teeth on a thirty metre stretch and ABDs up now!"

The platoons leapt into action. The last fight had given them no more than a few moments to prepare, but now they could bring new hardware to the table. The men pulled out boxes from the side and under trays of the trucks. They threw them down on the roads up ahead. The devices automatically created dug out trenches with earthwork barriers and tank traps.

The technology had cost a fortune to develop and the devices they used were equally as expensive. Never in their military's history had they had need for their usage. A platoon would take half a day to dig a trench and ground up earthworks, but these could do it in less than an hour. Better still, they could do so on any surface. Drawing anything from ground, from earth to concrete, they could create highly defensive positions in an astonishing time.

"Take up positions in the buildings! I want ARMALs on the roofs, deploy motors, set up a firing arc on this route. Let's give these bastards hell!" Jones shouted.

Chandra stepped back to his position after barking similar orders to the company she previously commanded.

"Captain, I have ordered A and B Companies to hold the southern limits as long as they can, this will be our last line of defence for the city. If they get past us here, the armour is finished."

"Girard having a hard time?"

"He's just about holding, but sounds like the enemy have brought up heavier equipment that we are yet to see. He might last a while in his current positions, but only if we can hold the rear."

Jones took the Major's arm and led her out of earshot of any of the men.

"We are digging our own graves here, Major. The only exit point we have left is the road to Morlaix to the east and we are getting dangerously close to be encircled."

"I am well aware of that, Captain, as is Brigadier Dupont."

"So he intends to leave us here to die?"

"No, Captain. The brass has accepted that our armour will never leave this place, they are organising a mass airlift as we speak. They only ask that we hold out as long as possible to keep the enemy from advancing further east while they amass forces."

Jones sighed in relief. He was beginning to lose faith in their leaders, now at least they had a plan. Their attention was quickly turned to a soaring sound of powerful engines to the west, followed by explosions in the city. They looked up to see the familiar blurred outlines of the camouflaged ships of the invaders flying by overhead. The city shook with the tremors of whatever bombs they had just dropped. They could only imagine the pounding the French armour was taking.

* * *

Taylor still sat uneasily amongst the top brass in the General's Command Centre. He never wanted the responsibility of sitting at a desk and making decisions that affected countries. The Major was a combat soldier. His rear was going numb and his knees beginning to ache. It was a clammy and humid room, but that may have just been the tension of the situation.

For all of his gruelling combat and physical training, Mitch had never felt so fatigued as he had done in this room. He looked again at the scanner, showing the flight trajectory of thousands of aircraft.

"What's our status?" asked Smith.

"Our boys are fifteen minutes out from target," said White.

The next step of the U.S. forces had been a massive aerial strike. No longer had their leaders fretted about small strikes or testing the water. They had amassed more fighters and bombers for one single mission that had been seen since a world war. Where a dozen missiles failed, thousands of aircraft could succeed, or at least that was the principle.

"Do we have any idea if we can shoot their craft down?"

Smith asked.

"This is a new experience for us all, we can only do the best under difficult circumstances. Our boys have faced off against these bastards. Major Taylor was able to bring down their soldiers and they aren't invulnerable. We'll keep hitting these bastards until they go down!" shouted White.

"General White, may I have a word with you in private?" asked Taylor.

The General nodded, he'd never been interrupted in the middle of an operation before, but he had quickly come to trust the Major. Not only that he knew he had to open his mind to new ideas. Both men were glad to get to their feet and stretch their weary bodies. White led Taylor into a small office next to the command room. They happily stood as they straightened their backs.

"General, we have to entertain the possibility that this mission will fail. Either because their aerial defences will be highly effective or our bombs are too ineffective."

"What are you suggesting, Major?"

"We know two things right now, we have had some success in ground combat, we just need bigger guns. We also know that France and Spain are taking a beating. I suggest we re-equip as best we can with heavy weapons and amass for a large scale infantry strike."

"At what location, Major?"

"Strike right at them. The EUA forces are fighting on mainland Europe to the east. If we strike directly at

Tartaros with substantial forces, we open a second front and take the fight to them. It should alleviate the pressure on Europe and allow them a chance to push back."

The General shook his head. He always knew in the back of his mind that a large-scale ground deployment could be possible, he'd just tried to not think about it.

"The last thing I want to do is put tens of thousands of troops into a warzone, but if it has to be done, so be it. Let us just be thankful that we're not having to fight on our own soil."

"Yes, Sir."

"Major, I am giving you permission to leave. We are not making any final decisions until we see the result of the air attack, but let's get started on sorting out the weapon situation. We still have a lot of weapons in store from fifty years ago, considered excessive for the modern day peace we enjoyed until so recently. Get to the armoury stores, you have permission to take and use anything you need, I am giving you the highest security clearance."

"I appreciate it, General, I will do my best to equip my company with the best equipment I can find, but we'll need to a equip a great many more men in the coming weeks."

"I hear you, Major. Sort through everything we have, equip your men and get a report to me by the end of the day on urgent operational requirements. Anything we need we'll put into immediate production or purchase."

"Yes, Sir. Thank you, Sir."

"Now, I have a mission to oversee, get to it, and God help us all."

Major Taylor saluted the General before taking his leave. He was grateful to get away from the high stress atmosphere of the Command Centre. Despite the risks involved, he would rather take a combat mission any day than return there.

He left the building and lifted his communicator, calling his company base. He requested Captain Friday and Sergeant Silva. He could not afford to remove too many of the command staff at any one time, but he also knew how vital it was to source new equipment. The armoury was a ten-minute drive across the base. He flagged down the first passing jeep.

The driver immediately recognised the Major and was keen to help. With his rank the man had little choice but to assist him, but he could have made it difficult, quoting procedure. The fact was that Taylor had become a minor celebrity on the base, the man who survived the Moon invasion and rescued their Prime Minister.

To Taylor the Moon mission was a disaster. But compared to much of what was happening on Earth it had at least succeeded in part. The driver, a young corporal, was eager to discuss the action he'd seen up there but it was a sad reminder of the events for the officer. Rolling up outside the armoury, Friday, Silva and also Parker were already there. Taylor was surprised that they were able to get there so quickly.

"How long have you been here, Captain?"

"A while, Sir."

"But I only called you here ten minutes ago."

"Sir, the company needs some hardware, we've been trying to convince them to give it to us all morning, but I fear anymore and we'll be escorted away."

Taylor grinned. His troops did not fear combat, they only loathed the idea of returning to it without the equipment they needed.

"The time for waiting is over, Captain, I have been given unlimited access and authority to draw whatever I wish, as well as to compile a report on recommended equipment for urgent operational requirements for the whole division."

"Right!" shouted Silva.

The Major continued on with the three others at his back. They waked right up to the guard entrance to the armouries. It was obvious that they had been putting up with the exploits of Captain Friday for some time, and had finally lost.

"Major Taylor?" the guard asked.

"Yeah."

"General White has authorised you full access to the stores and ordered our personnel to co-operate fully."

Taylor studied the man more intently, a sergeant. He

was certainly a man with no field experience, but a lot in administration. He had a scornful expression on his face, hating the fact that he had been forced to allow the others to pass.

The huge shutters of the massive structure opened. They were wide enough for a lorry to be driven through. The four marines stepped inside, stopping in amazement. Racks that were thirty metres high stretched as far back as they could see. None of them had ever seen the stores. All ammunition was delivered to and kept in battalion stores.

After the many great wars of the last century, much of the hardware had been put aside as it was considered unnecessary for a world that lived for the most part in peace. A corporal in combats came up to them, leaving the guard on duty at the front of the building.

"Welcome, gentlemen, I am Corporal Weaver. The General says you need some guns."

"Damn right, Corporal. We need personal arms. High explosive and armour penetration are the most important qualities. Last fight we had we simply didn't pack enough punch."

"Yes, Sir, a few things come to mind."

Weaver led them to an opening in the storage crates where several sofas were set up with a TV and a fridge.

"This where you spend your work hours?" asked Taylor.

"Only when the work runs out, Major."

Mitch laughed. The man clearly made the most of

his position, but he was also organised and efficient. He knew some officers would take issue with the Corporal's approach to aspects of his job, but he was only interested in the end result.

"Make yourself comfortable, Major, I'll be back with a selection of what we've got ASAP."

"Thank you, Corporal."

The Major and his marines took a seat as the Corporal hurried off about his business. Before any of them could open their mouths to speak a word, Taylor's communicator buzzed. He answered, it was General White.

"Major, the aerial attack has not gone as we had hoped. Our fighters have been met with heavy resistance and the bombing runs are not doing enough damage, not enough to make a difference."

"Sorry to hear that, General."

"Major, we can no longer sit by and fight from a distance, it's time to put men on the ground. That means I need you to work even faster than intended. I want a list of equipment recommendations for infantry forces in my hand within the next two hours. Understand this, Major, you're going to be entering a warzone, but without the industry and war machine working with you, you'll get nowhere!"

"Understood, General, over and out."

CHAPTER SEVEN

Four men stumbled into the room where Kelly sat, they carried one badly wounded man between them. The old Commander looked on with a woeful expression. Seeing his people die was a heart wrenching experience, but he knew that he could not win any victories without losses.

"Sir, we took down two of the bastards, but we have two dead and two wounded. We can't win with this sort of attrition, there's just not enough of us."

Kelly looked around the room at the bedraggled forces. They had adopted an old underground research facility as their new base. So far it was unknown to the enemy forces. A hundred men and women lay about the facility, tightly packed in. Thousands more were crammed into any safe place that could be found.

The regular missions into the building above ground were risky, but a necessary risk in order to continue rescuing survivors and foraging for supplies. It was apparent that many of the alien forces had left the Moon to assist in the battle for Earth, but there was still more than enough of a force to stop them from fighting in open combat.

"We need to contact Earth, we need their help. Guns, ammunition and food. Without it we are dead," said Kelly.

"What are they going to do for us? You saw what the Earth forces did when we were attacked! They turned tail and ran!"

Kelly looked at the angry soldier, Private Doyle of the MDF, who had risen to commander of a section simply through battlefield casualties."

"I will remind you, Doyle, that many UEN soldiers still fight and die beside us!"

"Not by choice, they'd have got out if they could!"

Kelly got up and stormed across the room, shouting at the man.

"Don't you think we'd all have gotten out if we knew what was coming? We defend these lands for the people, not for the damn land!"

Doyle looked sheepish. He knew he'd been an idiot, but it was a hard fact to stomach or admit. The Moon inhabitants had become hugely attached to their lands, despite few Earth dwellers understanding the appeal.

"We have a steady supply of air down here with plenty of processors feeding into the old bunkers we are using. However, we were never equipped for war. We have too few guns, an ever dwindling supply of ammunition and food is running out quickly."

"You think anyone down there can or will be willing to help, Sir?"

"Yes, I do. But if they're not aware of these hardships we are facing it is unlikely they will, so I cannot guarantee we will get any assistance. But I'm confident that if they knew they would do everything in their power to help us."

"I could get a signal out," said Lewis.

Kelly shot a glance at the communications officer, a capable man who had never experienced field duties.

"Are you certain?"

"If at least some of the equipment is still undamaged, then yeah, I can do it."

"Where would you need to be?"

"At one of the comms stations, nearest is just above the surface from here on the third floor of the library."

"Good, then let's not waste any time, prep anything you need, I'll assemble a message so there is no time wasted. Doyle, get your wounded taken care of, but return immediately with a full section, draw troops from wherever you have to."

"Yes, Sir."

Doyle rushed off to carry out his orders. The demoralised young man had seen a glimmer of hope and was chasing it with all his energy. Kelly turned back to the comms officer who looked uneasy. He was impressed at the man's courage in volunteering, but he could see the fear in his face and body language.

"Lewis, what else do we need?"

"Just me, get me to those rooms with the message you want to send and pray everything still works!"

Ten minutes later the men were assembled and ready to move. They strapped on their body armours. The experiences they'd in combat had shown the armours to be far less effective than against man-made weapons. But they could still save a man from glancing blows, as well as fragmentation and trauma from explosions that some of the pulse weapons caused.

Kelly felt foolish in his armour, too old to be wearing it and too old to be fighting. Despite this, he would not ask the men to risk what he would not. Getting that signal out could be the single most important thing they did for survival and he wanted to ensure it went to plan. Twelve men were all that were going up into the surface buildings. They had many more capable fighters, but they couldn't fight the enemy in open combat. They had become reliant on staying out of contact or ambushing one or two of the Mechs at a time.

"All ready?" he asked.

The men nodded. He looked around the room to see civilians and soldiers alike staring at them. Their faces were blank, still in shock. Many of them had seen friends, family and neighbours killed by the invading creatures. He knew he could not leave without giving them some hope.

"Listen up! All of you!"

The room was near silent before, but now you could hear a pin drop.

"We are going to get help from Earth! I am confident that if they can find a way, they will help us! We didn't come down here to die, we came here to survive! We'll beat these sons of bitches. I know you have lost a lot, we all have, but we still have each other! We will survive and we will win!"

There was no response, no cheering, the people were still too shocked to show any major emotion. He could see that a few faces looked doubtful, but many more had just a faint touch of hope.

"Martinez, if I don't return, you're in charge."

Kelly had known the officer for many years. He liked the man and trusted him with many things, but knew that he wouldn't be capable of leading them to survival, let alone victory. Despite this, he had no better choice. He made the gesture out of procedure rather than anything else.

"Let's go!"

They strode out of the room towards one of the access tunnels they used to get up to the surface structure. A ladder led up to a small storage room on the ground floor of the library building above. The underground access tunnels had been carefully hidden and forgotten by most overtime. They had been sealed off for government and military use only.

Kelly climbed the ladder first, lifting the hatch that was well concealed under the carpet of the small room. He raised it only a few centimetres, listening for the sound of the huge Mechs constantly patrolling the buildings above ground. The area was quiet, a welcome piece of news. He lifted it higher and climbed out into the room, followed by his team which completely filling it.

"Put the hatch back down," he whispered.

Cautiously opening the door, the Commander stepped out into the corridor of the ground floor of the library. He had become very familiar with the structure years ago, when he regularly visited in order to meet various groups to discuss the documentation of the colonisation of the Moon. Libraries had seen a major resurgence since people wished to publically discuss the things they read.

The lights were still on. The colony would run without any maintenance for years to come. The highly developed nuclear power source would keep the power on, as well as oxygen and water processing going almost indefinitely. He stepped towards the staircase, not wanting to risk activating the elevators, even though they were working.

The building was eerily silent and as they reached the stairway it immediately became clear that every sound they made echoed through the tall stairwell. Kelly had seen enough of the enemy to know that he never wanted to see them again. The thought of going above ground scared him more than anything in his life, but to do nothing would condemn every surviving colonist to death.

* * *

"Get down!" shouted Jones.

An energy pulse from one of the enemy vehicle's mounted cannons smashed into the building above them, rocking the structure. Glass and debris crashed all around them. The body armour suits were all that kept the men from sustaining serious injury. The Captain was momentarily stunned by the deafening crash of the building collapsing around him. Clawing his way to his feet, he shook off the dust covering his body.

"Get on the guns! Keep firing!"

Charlie ran along the line of the corridor that had been their firing position. Several of his men were stumbling about trying to regain their composure. His hearing began to recover and the first sounds were the French guns around their position.

"Where are you going, Sir?" shouted Saunders.

"I need to talk to Girard!"

The comms equipment had been jammed soon after the siege had begun. Jones had been expecting this from the very beginning after Taylor had warned him about the incident on the Moon. The lack of communication created a number of problems for the ground forces which they will still unable to overcome.

The Captain ducked and weaved along the corridor as explosions continued as his troops fired back into the street. Jones had read about such vicious city warfare in the history books, but he didn't think he'd personally ever have to experience it. The modern armies existed really as a police force and acted only in the intervention of small military conflicts.

Jones reached the door of the building where they had been stationed. He looked into the street where several French tanks were stationed and firing as quickly as they could. Debris from the buildings above swept across the street. Charlie moved forward but stopped abruptly as a section of concrete large enough to crush a man smashed in front of him. He immediately went down on one knee, not to present a target to the enemy. He looked to his left where the fortifications were built, the enemy had already reached the perimeter and the two companies in his battalion had fled back to their positions.

To his right he could see Girard shouting at two of his officers by his command vehicle. Things were not going well. Jones got to his feet and ran along the rubble-strewn road keeping his head low until he reached the Colonel. Just as he got there the two officers were given their final grilling and sent on their way. As he neared the vehicle he could see Major Chandra was next to the Colonel.

"Captain Jones, how goes the southern defences?"

"Not great, Colonel, we are giving them hell. The narrow corridor is giving a good field of fire, but we're burning through ammo."

"Captain, that is exactly the discussion we were just having," said Chandra.

"We're holding just a square kilometre of the city centre but it's becoming more difficult to hold. However, the city reserve ammunition stores remain intact," Girard added.

"Where are they stored, Sir?"

"In a secret location beneath a building half a kilometre to the north."

"Outside our positions, Colonel?"

"That's right, Captain. Jones, as you know, our communication signals are being jammed. The last news we received was that an airlift was being organised to pull us out, but it's taking time to organise."

"Why, Sir? Surely they could evac us within an hour or two?"

"Not that anyone is saying it, Captain, but it seems like we are the only forces to have held out. We are providing valuable time for the civilians to flee and the rest of our forces to amass."

Jones shook his head. They were buying time for everyone else with their lives. Ultimately he knew it was what they were paid to do as soldiers, but he never thought that it would actually be asked of them.

"Captain, we could potentially be here until tomorrow, but our ammunition stores will only last another couple of hours at most."

"I am getting the message, Major, what can I do?"

"We need a company to volunteer, I am hoping that would be you, Jones."

The Captain knew he really had no choice in the matter. Not only that, but he was sick of taking a pounding in their southern positions.

"I'm organising some armour for you now, Captain. You'll have three heavy tanks and three APCs. Between them they'll be able to carry more than enough ammunition to keep us in the fight."

"What sort of resistance do we expect, Sir?"

"I have planned a route for you to take which hopefully should present as few problems as possible. Ultimately, Captain, we simply don't know. Do whatever you can to bring those supplies back, without them we are finished!"

Jones thought hard about the situation, realising the desperate situation they were in and what weight was being placed on his shoulders. He saluted the two other officers before running off to gather his company. He'd lost so many men, but now he was worrying less about how many casualties he was taking, and more about how many he could save.

* * *

"Major! The General is requesting you immediately!" shouted Friday.

The Major was stood with a grin on his face and a revolving grenade launcher in his arms. The weapon had long been decommissioned by Earth force militaries. It had been considered completely at odds with the modern policing actions that troops carried out. The eight shot, 30mm launcher fired formidable armour piercing or high explosive rounds. Taylor's face quickly turned to concern as the order was relayed.

"Any idea as to what it's regarding?"

"No, Sir, the General wants only you and STAT!"

Taylor put the launcher down on the table. Up ahead was the burning wreck of an obsolete armoured vehicle they had been using for testing their new weapons. Alongside the launcher was an array of heavy and unusual weaponry.

"Time to cut this short, gentlemen! Captain, I want you to complete the report for urgent operational requirements. Silva and Parker, grab as much of this kit as you can and get it to our company barracks immediately. I'll be back soon to introduce the new tools to our men!"

His troops leapt into action as the Major rushed out to where his jeep was parked. The base was still a hive of activity. A number of troops had stopped to observe the tests they were carrying out. Everyone could see that this was a prelim to all out war. Many of the marines on duty stared at the Major as he came out of the stores warehouse, desperate to ask him questions. They all saluted as he passed them. There was no longer anyone on the base of any rank that didn't recognise Taylor.

The heat in the base was reaching unbearable levels, compounded by the mass activity and necessity of bearing of arms. Taylor wiped his brow and shook off a handful of sweat as he raced across the base. Sweat pockets filled his uniform, only disguised by the disruptive camouflage pattern that he was wearing. He rushed into the operations room without opposition from the guards.

"Major!"

"Sir, the report is on its way."

"Good work, Taylor, but that's not why I called you here. We just received a signal from the Moon colony!"

"Is it genuine, Sir? I didn't think anyone could survive that onslaught."

"Never underestimate Kelly, we served together a long time ago. If anyone can survive on that occupied hell hole, it will be him!"

"Then he is alive, Sir?"

"And kicking. The surviving forces and civilians have moved underground into a series of bunkers, research centres and tunnels. It seems the survivors are in their tens of thousands."

"Christ, and we left them there!"

"Major, you had your orders and you carried them out. This is not about right and wrong. We needed the Prime

Minister and yourself back on Earth. You could have done nothing to evacuate their numbers!"

Taylor nodded. He felt shame for the loss of so many lives, but he knew that there was nothing more they could have done.

"The Moon has become a guerrilla war. Colonel Visser is dead, but many of the soldiers stationed there, as well as the militia, fight on. Kelly is organising regular missions to find supplies, but they face one big problem. Even when they can get those bastards alone, it's still a hell of a fight to bring them down."

"Yes, Sir, I can fully understand that."

"I refuse to leave those poor bastards to die on that rock. Our forces will continue to amass ready for a major ground assault, but until that time, your new task is to get supplies to Kelly."

"General White, we are facing worldwide disaster! We must look to our own defences!" shouted Smith.

"We will face our own battles in the days to come, but I will not and cannot leave our people to die up there!"

"Sir, I can fully appreciate the sentiment, but last time we were there we left with our tail between our legs. We can't outrun or outgun their ships!"

"Not with our technology, Major, but with theirs we can."

"Sir?"

"Our tech guys have been going over two enemy vessels

which we have captured in lightly damaged condition."

"What happened to their occupants?" asked Taylor.

"That is a subject for another time. From now on you will be liaising with the research and tech teams handling the alien vessels. You will also be organising the Moon supply drop. We cannot send troops up there, but food and weapons are the priority. I want you to find pilots that are both capable and crazy enough to fly such a mission, and ensure that the cargo contains weapons that will give them a fighting chance. Understood?"

"Yes, Sir."

The Major's grin stretched across his face. Leaving the Moon colonists was the most difficult decision of his life, but now he was being given a chance to redeem himself.

"I have assigned you my driver, Sergeant Gibbons. You can bring your company officers of NCOs in on this programme, but beyond that, this is between us, Major. Do what you have to do."

"Yes, Sir!"

Taylor turned quickly and ran out of the room to be greeted by Gibbons who had obviously already been briefed on the situation.

"Sir, I am here to take you to the research facility."

"Not quite yet, Sergeant, we have a few people to pick up!"

The two men jumped into their jeep and stormed away from the Command Centre, making their way for the

Major's barracks at speeds far beyond those allowed on base. Not a single marine dared confront their breach of base rules, not even the MPs. Major Taylor had always been an important officer on base, leading one of the most advanced and experienced companies in the United States Armies. But now he was not just important, but known. No one would stand in his way.

They reached the barracks and Taylor leapt off, telling the Sergeant to stay put. He rushed into his office to see that Captain Friday was already writing out the reports for the release and request of the hardware they had tested.

"Captain, bring that with you, we have a new task on our hands!"

Friday leapt from his chair and was out the door with his datapad in a split second. Taylor had always appreciated the fact that the Captain never questioned his orders and never dragged his heels. Suarez strolled across the parade square as they jumped into the vehicle.

"Lieutenant! You're in charge until we return!" Taylor ordered.

The Major looked back to Captain Friday who was in the back of the Jeep

"Captain, we're en route to oversee a special mission, I need you to contact Eddie Rains and tell him to meet us at..."

Taylor looked to the General's driver who was at the wheel.

"Where are we headed, Sergeant?"

"Hangar 89."

"Got it, Major."

"And tell him to bring three capable pilots with him!" Taylor added.

It was half an hour before they arrived at the giant hangar that was situated a way out from the base and on the edge of a vehicle-testing zone. It was an isolated and desolate area with vast open plains surrounding it. The three men stopped their vehicle outside, the small jeep was dwarfed by the huge storage facility.

The hangar had little sign of activity, with just one small guardroom built onto the front. It appeared to be a sleepy old structure, forgotten and lost in time, in lieu of the modern structures they now operated from.

"I thought this place went inactive twenty years ago?" said Friday.

"I guess some things are just above our pay grade," replied Taylor.

A vehicle approached from the direction they had come. The Major turned to see the familiar sight of Eddie Rains' faded red bandana wrapped around his head as he sat up on the back of the vehicle. Dust kicked up all around them and into their eyes as the vehicle slid to a halt and the pilots leapt out. Ever the gung ho rule breakers, it was if they simply rebelled as a matter of tradition.

"You got a job for us, Major?" Rains called.

"That's right, Eddie, it'll be wild, dangerous, and you'd be an idiot to accept it!"

The Lieutenant turned to his friends with a smile.

"You called the right men, Major!"

Two men appeared from the guard station and they were well equipped. Far from the old and out of shape old soldiers that were employed to guard most storage depots, they were young and fit. They wore full battle attire and didn't lack an ounce of professionalism.

"Welcome to Hangar 89, gentlemen, home to every secret project and finding since this base opened."

"You're not just the General's driver are you, Sergeant?"

"No, Sir, I am his liaison to this facility and advisor on all matters involving it."

"A lot of responsibility for a Sergeant."

"I retired a Major, Sir, then worked for the CIA. I was posted to him with the rank of Sergeant and as the General's driver as to maintain anonymity in my work."

The security guards looked at them from a distance, studying every element of the men who stood before them. They'd already been given clearance for the facility, and the guards never moved closer than ten metres. A large door opened in the front of the hangar that was large enough for a truck to drive through, but still tiny in comparison to the vast bay doors.

"The hangar is close to half a kilometre long, with three underground levels and two above ground. What is of interest to us today, Major, are the captured enemy vessels."

"What condition are they in?"

"They aren't flight worthy if that's what you're asking, but there's plenty of interesting material to salvage from them."

Gibbons led them through the huge entrance and a temporary corridor existing only to hide whatever the building housed from the outside world. It took a few moments for their eyes to adjust from the striking light of the day to the artificially lit warehouse. Before them were the two craft as the General had said, evidently the latest acquisitions in the hangar. The room stretched as far as they could see with at least a hundred staff members in sight.

"These two craft were captured soon after the Moon base fell. Our intelligence suggests that they were advance patrol ships. One was hit by our fighters and crash landed in the desert, the other was struck by one of our destroyer's EMP pulse defences when it entered its grid zone."

"Man, I'd love to take one out for a spin," said Rains.

"Well that's not far from the reality of the situation, Lieutenant. The plan is to retrofit the alien engine tech to something you lot can fly. We need something fast enough to outrun whatever they've got so that you lot can get to the Moon and back."

"There are survivors, Sir?"

"That's right, Rains, lots of them. We need to deliver food and weapons to the survivors who are still putting up a fight there."

One of the other pilots jumped into the conversation before the Major could continue.

"But we're aerial pilots, Sir, space isn't our domain."

"Well that is true, son," said the Sergeant. "However, we need combat pilots for this mission, not space haulers. Now, every minute we waste puts more lives at risk."

"You heard the man, Rains. Our task is to get supplies to the Moon survivors as quickly as possible. In my book, that means tomorrow. Our task is to get two vessels kitted out with the enemy engine technology and en route by then, with you boys at the stick."

"It's a tall order, Sir," Rains replied. "It takes experts months and years to design aircraft, how are we going to manage it by tomorrow?"

"Look, we aren't designing anything from scratch. This is a bodge job. We use the smallest space worthy vessels available and strap on those alien engines, job done!"

"It's a crazy idea, Major, but what we come out with will be badass!" shouted Rains.

Eddie stepped down the ramps to look over the damaged alien vessels that were laid out across the floor. He was admiring the fuselages that didn't resemble anything he was familiar with.

"You think it can be done, Eddie?"

"Damn right, Sir, you want us to build a monster, that idea tickles me just a little."

"Right then, get to work. Whatever you build doesn't have to be pretty. It just has to work. I will arrange what cargo you'll need to take, but the experts here have already found the best ships to start work with, get on it!"

Eddie lifted his arm in an almost comical salute with a broad grin across his face. Anyone else would have been beside themselves if they'd been asked to do what Eddie was, but he found the challenge entertaining.

Taylor had Captain Friday assemble a viable supply list that night. A list that would be vital for the survivors as well as feasible to carry on the new ships they were building. He left Eddie, his pilots and the tech guys to work that day and night, knowing there was nothing more he could do.

It was another uneasy night for the Major, knowing the pressure he was under to succeed in what could only be called an insane mission. Yet another night he slept alone for the few uncomfortable hours that he could manage. He had never longed for Eli Parker's company. They'd fallen into bed when the time was right. Now he was beginning to wish she was home to greet him, to have some comfort in difficult times.

Waking up in a sticky sweat, Taylor pulled his uniform on as he begrudgingly imagined the results of their project. He had faith in Eddie Rains, even if he did resemble a drug-crazed hippy. The Lieutenant was one of the best pilots and most competent men he'd ever known. He just didn't like to be seen as such.

The horn on Gibbon's vehicle blared out violently outside before he'd even got his gun on his side. It was a make or break day for the supply drops to the stricken colonists. Many thousands of lives were depending on him and the project, he only prayed that they could succeed. Mitch ran down to the vehicle below, sweat already dripping through his clothes.

"Fine day for it, Major!" shouted Gibbons.

"If we were on the beach, there was no war and we had a bar full of ice cold beers, I might agree with you, Sergeant!"

Taylor climbed aboard, his concern transparent despite the fact that he tried to hide it beneath locker room humour.

"Don't worry, Major, I've already been down to the hangar. Your boys have been working straight through the night, they've done more than anyone could have expected of them."

The Major shook his head in gratitude and relief.

"Right then, let's see it for ourselves!"

Approaching the hangar across the long open plain, Mitch could see that the huge hangar bay doors were wide open for all to see. It was perhaps the first time ever during daylight hours for a century.

"Nothing to hide anymore, Major. In a matter of hours, every son of a bitch on this base is gonna know about our creations, no point wasting time hiding now."

"You really think they are gonna work?"

Gibbons nodded with a nervous expression on his face.

"I damn well hope so, Major."

Pulling up outside the doors, Taylor could see that Eddie was walking around the nose of the vessel they'd been working on, admiring his work or perhaps inspecting it. There were two ships, one in front of the other. They were Lampeter class 'spaceboats'. A small but armoured ship capable of carrying a hundred soldiers and equipment, or plenty of supplies. It was intended to act as a military transport and supply vessel.

A fraction of the size of the Deveron they had previously travelled on to the Moon, and substantially faster. It was mainly intended to act as a fast deployment vessel during any public disturbances, allowing earth forces to rapidly deploy troops to the Moon or any of the Space stations.

"You like her, Sir?"

"If it does the job, Eddie!"

The quirky pilot turned to greet the Major.

"It's like the old fast boats the drug cartels used to outrun the authorities back in the day."

Taylor looked around the fuselage of the vessel, it had two alien engines fitted, one slung under the belly, the other sitting on the top.

"We've kept her original engines, Sir. She was a fast bird to begin with, probably not enough to outrun what we're facing, but a good start. With these wondrous beasts bolted onto her and she'll outfly anything we've ever seen!"

"I certainly hope so. How much of the cargo capacity have you lost adding these things?"

"Nothing at all, Major. The energy sources those alien bastards use are fascinating, everything we have fitted is external. The tech guys here have worked out the engine tech, it'll be a while till they understand the weapon systems and that chameleon tech they have."

"So you think this can work? What's your ETA?"

"This baby is ready, Sir, other one is having finishing touches. Captain Friday already has our cargo en route, I hope to be in the air in two hours."

"Isn't that a little premature, Lieutenant, you haven't even tested these things yet?"

"We've tested everything we need to, Sir. The ships run just as they used to, the alien engines fire up and work as they should, any flight runs would just draw attention to ourselves."

The Major nodded. He didn't like the situation, but knew that under the wartime conditions they faced, some risks had to be taken.

"Lieutenant, I'll leave you to it, let me know when you're ready to fly."

"Yes, Sir!"

Eddie ran off in a hive of excitement as he went back to work on his precious new ships. The Major climbed back aboard Gibbons' vehicle and continued on to General White's Command Centre. He walked in to find a familiar sight. Nothing had changed since his last visit, other than the enemy lines having pushed further into France and Spain.

"Major! Give us an update on your situation," said White.

"Sir. The supply boats will be ready for lift-off in two hours. Additionally, Captain Friday has completed our report on operational requirements and further procurement."

"Well done, Major, I have already received your report. While I congratulate you on your work with the alien technology, your report can be described as nothing but farfetched."

"Major, you are asking for the manufacture of tens of thousands of new weapons, perhaps more, how can our country pay for this?" asked Smith.

Taylor looked at the General dismayed. In previous years he'd gotten used to budget constraints and concerns about overspending, but he had imagined that they were beyond that now.

"Sir, we are no longer a peacetime country that is maintaining our forces. We are at war with an enemy far superior to us, we need every advantage we can get in this fight."

"Major, we have the best trained and equipped army in the world, is that not enough?"

"No, General Smith, it isn't. The EUA forces in France and Spain have just as good equipment as our boys, and they're taking a beating. Best equipment and army in the world accounts for nothing when we face an otherworldly enemy, Sir."

"You took the bastards down, Major, you didn't need anything more than you had!"

"All due respect, General. You didn't see them. You didn't fight them. I lost many more marines than we took down of theirs. You want to play a numbers game and hope we have more men to throw away than them, fine! But I suggest you grab a rifle and join the tally!"

Taylor threw his chair back and jumped to his feet, storming from the room without recognition of his superiors. He was not one to be disrespectful, but when their leaders were not taking the lives of the men seriously, it was a hard thing to endure. Any one of the Generals could have had him disciplined for the way he acted towards them, but none had the heart.

Striding out into the parking lot, Mitch leapt into Gibbons' vehicle and signalled for him to go on before anyone could stop them. Taylor looked back at the Command Centre as they sped off towards the hangar, but nobody appeared to chase him. Taylor only had two things on his mind at that moment, the lives of the Moon colonists and his European counterparts.

Taylor passed anxiously along the lines of marines continually on high alert and patrolling the base. It seemed that more than ever was resting on his shoulders. The Moon extraction mission of the Prime Minister was an ambitious task for the Major's company, but still within their remit. Organising a highly dangerous and never before planned supply drop to the Moon under wartime conditions, using technology that they had never seen before, was a wholly different affair.

As their vehicle rolled up towards the hangar they could see that the two ships had already been pulled out onto the old derelict runway. With the huge alien engines fitted and rudimentary landing gear, they were an odd hybrid of ideas. It looked as if they were built from components that were a hundred years apart in design.

Beside the vehicles were trucks full of the weapons and ammunition that Captain Friday had organised. Taylor had selected a hundred of the 30mm revolving grenade launchers to be sent to the Moon colonists. Armour piercing rounds were supplied in huge quantities, being the only rounds suitable for their environment.

Eddie Rains stood with his arms crossed admiring the work going on before him. It was clear that he enjoyed the attention he got for dressing a long way from regulations, but Taylor was glad of his confidence and composure.

"Lieutenant, give me an update!" shouted Taylor.

He barked his orders before the vehicle had even come to a stop, leaping off as he finished.

"Last load, Major, we're good to go in five. In fact its time for me to load up, Sir!"

"Good luck, Eddie, I pray you make it there and back, for their sake and yours."

He reached out his hand to the flight Lieutenant. Rains took it with a grin on his face. Nothing could ever get the pilot down, at least he never showed it. He turned and climbed aboard the craft. It was far larger than his typical mission, but nothing he wasn't trained on. The extra power of the alien engines would make it feel more extreme than anything he'd ever flown. Taylor knew he must be scared, but he appreciated that Eddie put on a brave face.

The trucks beside the spacecraft cleared out as the doors clamped shut. Each ship had only two pilots and no other crew. They could neither afford nor risk any more personnel. They also needed the maximum capacity for supplies going to the colonists. There were no clearance lights, no control tower and no one to see them off beside Taylor and a select few staff involved in the operation.

Standing a few hundred metres back, Taylor watched Eddie climb into the pilot's seat in the nose cone of the ship. Each of the vessels was decked out with an adequate selection of weapons controlled remotely by the pilot and co-pilot, but it was little relief when they knew the odds they faced. Speed was the essence of this mission.

Eddie and the other crew fired up the regular engines and the ships quickly lifted off in keeping with their reputation as exceptionally fast and agile vessels for their size. Powering up they lifted off and tilted up to the sky. The ships glimmered as the alien engines fired up and without warning they blasted off, faster than anything any of them had seen in their lives.

"Good luck, Eddie, to all of you!"

CHAPTER EIGHT

Captain Jones crept from the street corner to an alcove. They continued to their position ahead of the armoured column, having just past through the French lines. Charlie could see his men's nerves hung on a knife's edge. The guns continued to roar in the background as they carried on, their movements covered by the fire.

It was a long trip to the weapons depot, not in distance, but in time. Every step had to be carefully negotiated. With the equipment they had they could only hold off a light assault by the Mechs. Having armour was a relief to the infantry forces, but it was far too little against the odds they faced.

"Sir, the position is just fifty metres ahead," whispered Green.

The Lieutenant was pointing to a low building that appeared to be a substation, but was likely far more. Jones looked back to his men waiting for his command, but they were not at all keen in advancing any further.

"Get the armour surrounding the building, the APCs remain on the south side for loading, I want eyes on the roof ASAP."

The men immediately moved forward. Far from the lines of the EUA forces it was eerily quiet. The guns raged in the background but all around them was quiet, like sunrise before commuters had risen to go to work. The building was protected by nothing more than a wire fence and a locked door that presented little resistance to the troops. Captain Jones went into the building where he immediately found more doors. They were huge steel doors as tall as the building. A keypad entry system was at eye level. Fortunately the Colonel had already supplied Jones with the codes. He quickly tapped them in, sceptical as to whether they would even work. He wondered if anyone had accessed the building in a few decades, they were a reminder of the days of fragile peace amongst the major powers on Earth.

The keypad flashed as the doors prized opened twenty metres wide. They could see crates of weapons and ammunition. The rifles were obsolete compared to what they now used, but the ammunition was still the same.

"We're in business! Get the APCs up here and get to work!"

The first vehicle backed up against the structure as the

heavy tanks rolled on around the perimeter. The Captain had not yet seen the effectiveness of their armour against the invaders. However, by the fact that they still held Brest, he speculated that they had played a major part.

"Make sure we have eyes on all quarters! I want to know the second we hit any trouble!"

Jones pulled his rifle sling around until the weapon hung on his back and his hands were free. He reached out for the first crate, hauling it off the stack and towards the vehicle. Doctrine had taught him to never dig in with the labour of the rank and file, but experience had showed him that they didn't want to be in enemy territory a second longer than they had to.

* * *

"Taylor, give us an update!" shouted White.

"The boats are on the way as we speak, General, we expect them to hit the ground in thirty minutes."

"You think they'll deliver the goods and get out okay?"

"Yes, Sir."

"Then let's deal with the next shit storm at our door!"

"Sir?"

"A new front has opened in North Africa. Reports suggest that the African nations' forces have been pushed back at an alarming rate, along with the UEN forces stationed there. Spain is also falling at an alarming rate."

The General tapped his screen and brought up the latest map before them. It was received with a gasp as each of the top brass saw quite how fast the world was falling.

"Towns and cities are falling so quickly right now that we can barely keep track of the current lines, let alone get much intel!"

"What's our next step here, General?" asked Taylor.

"I want a full report from Moon colonists on the effectiveness of the weapons we are sending them. Meanwhile, relying on the reports you made for us, we are equipping as many of the units as possible."

"So we do nothing?"

"I will not risk ground troops until we have re-equipped as best as possible as per your recommendations, Major."

"And what about Europe? Africa? We are just going to let them all die?"

"At this stage we'd just be adding more bodies to the pile, Major. Let's make sure that when we move we have enough muscle to make a dent."

Taylor lowered his head. Yet more inaction and delaying on the General's part was a depressing and ever more common experience. He knew that every action would be on the General's shoulders, but he also knew that the time had come to act.

"I want reports the second those weapons have seen action, Major."

"Yes, Sir."

† ✳ ✳

Lt. Rains looked amazed at the readings on their equipment. He had been space trained as per regulations, but he never envisaged the speed at which they were blasting towards the Moon. Beside him sat Lieutenant Perez, who'd been his co-pilot for several years.

"Never thought to be in this seat, Eddie."

"We got the best seats in the house, my friend. Delivering help to the needy and riding in probably the fastest ship that has ever existed. We're having a blast!"

"Let's just hope its fast enough," Perez replied wearily.

The Moon colony was now in sight, a vast ugly city to their Earth dwelling eyes. Like Taylor, they could never understand why anyone would want to live there. They still had no idea on the sort of scanning and surveillance equipment the invaders used. They had never travelled into a combat situation without a thorough understanding of their enemy, let alone such a fear of them.

Speed and surprise were the only tools to hand for the few brave pilots rocketing towards the Moon at speed. Taylor had already predicted they would have an absolute maximum of five minutes on the ground before encountering trouble. Previous experience showed that they would have the guns to take on a small group of fighters, but not any great numbers.

The landing zone was a barren and desolate area a kilometre from the edge of the colony. To even the well-trained eye it was every bit as untouched by humanity as it appeared. To anyone who knew better, beneath the surface was a military bunker and tunnel system leading to various parts of the colony.

"What if we get hit by ground troops, Eddie? We haven't planned for that possibility."

"Then we're fucked. Planning has been as good as can be, now it's down to luck."

"Hardly reassuring!"

"If you wanted certainty, Perez, you should have worked at a desk."

Perez nodded with a grin. They both loved their work, the thrill of the high-speed combat aircraft and exhilaration they experienced through much of their work. Now for the first time ever their stomachs churned as their own mortality become uncomfortably apparent.

"This is it!" shouted Eddie.

The two craft tore across the lunar landscape at blinding speeds just a hundred metres above the surface.

"Be ready on the guns!"

"They better be ready for us!" screamed Perez.

Eddie closely watched the heads up display in the cockpit, carefully timing their rapid drop onto the landing zone. Just a hundred metres short of the target area, and still with no sign of life, he put the thrusters on full reverse bringing the ship to a sudden and violent landing exactly where he'd been told to land. All four of the men were still doubtful of the intel and the ability of the surviving colonists to be there waiting for them.

He immediately powered down the engines to silence the scene and draw as little attention to them as possible. They could only hope that their presence had gone unnoticed but they knew that was too much to hope for. Rains reached forward and tapped the display, bringing up the under slung cameras on the craft. For a moment they saw nothing but the same boring rocks that spread as far as the eye could see beyond the colony.

"Think we hit the right spot?" asked Perez.

"We hit the right co-ordinates, that's for sure."

"Great, suits fucked it up again..."

Before he could say another word the ground opened between the two vessels, just metres away from the landing sleds.

"Holy shit!"

The opening was thirty metres wide and disguised the man-made structure below. On the cameras they could see a platform rising to the surface with dozens of people suited up and ready to get to work.

"We are in business, Eddie!"

He hit the cargo doors as the massive platform rose to the level of their side doors. The pilots had been ordered to stay in their seats at all times. They wanted nothing more than to greet their comrades, but they had to be ready to leave or operate weapons at a moment's notice.

Eddie watched the screens intently, rocking back and forth with the stress and excitement of it all. Perez scanned the skies with his monitors and camera displays, sneaking a peak at the colonists every few seconds. They set on the supplies like a swarm. They were highly organised and efficient, just as the pilots had hoped, but never expected.

Rains typed into the display monitors in the docking bay, the only way they had to communicate with the colonists. His message read 'three minutes remaining'. A man on the decking bay looked up at their cameras and gave a nod in recognition.

"They're brave sons of bitches," said Perez.

"What else could they be?" replied Eddie.

"What ya mean?"

"With this enemy, you either run or you fight. They had no place to run."

"They could have just given up, accepting a quick death."

He nodded in acknowledgement. There was no doubt that it took balls to combat a vastly superior enemy when isolated from Earth. In just two minutes the colonists had shifted half of the payloads of the two ships, an impressive feat. Desperation was pushing them to work faster than any crew back at the base.

"Any sign of trouble?" asked Eddie.

"Nothing yet, but you know those bastards, damn bitch to see them. Plus we're exposed from every angle here."

"Just a little longer."

Perez's eyes shot across the cockpit glass in front of them.

"What the hell was that?"

"What? What did you see?" shouted Eddie.

"I don't know, maybe something."

He hit the keyboard violently, signalling for the ground crew to shift their butts. Perez's instincts were rarely wrong, a fact Eddie wished was not the case now.

"Be ready on the guns, this is gonna be a hot exit!"

"I never expected anything else. Riding with you is never boring, Eddie!"

Rains looked down at the screen, the colonists were unloading the last few of the crates. One of them walked up to the camera he was watching them on. He looked directly into the lens and held his thumb up with a grateful nod, followed by a salute. Eddie was as chilled out as any man could be, but the sentiment brought tears to his eyes.

He knew it would likely to be a fight to get home, but for them it was just in and out, back to a safe home. For the Lunar colonists it was going to be a war with no end in sight. He typed one last message into the display box, 'good luck friend'.

"We've got incoming!" Perez shouted.

Rains took one last look down at the screen to see

the man step off their docking ramp. He hammered the retract switch, knowing he could not spend a second longer considering their allies on the ground. From now on the only mission was to survive.

"Weapons hot! Let's get off this rock!" shouted Eddie.

He fired up and put power down to all engines. The craft hopped off the surface with immense speed, lurching forward so quickly that it caught Eddie off guard.

"Whoa! Easy now!"

"They're closing on us!" shouted Perez.

"Give them everything we've got!"

Perez squinted to distinguish the enemy ships from the terrain. He was forced to use the manual targeting pads, something he'd only ever done in simulation and training exercises. As he looked across the sky in his wall of monitors he gasped at the sheer number of anomalies in the sky.

"Jesus Christ! Get us the hell out of here!"

Rains could see through the cockpit window that the vessels were closing in. Perez opened fire immediately as they began to build speed. The enemy fired their energy weapons, narrowly missing them.

"Damn this is one fast son of a bitch!"

"Whoa, Eddie, yeah!"

The enemy fired once more, but it was too late. Their smaller craft, with far higher power output, were vastly superior in speed to the enemy ships.

"Didn't think I'd see the day! We gotta get some more of these babies!" Eddie laughed.

Rain's broad grin swiftly turned to a grimace as he thought about the colonists. They were free and clear, able to outrun their enemy, but it was a whole different story for Kelly and his troops. They could only pray that the supply drop would go some way to giving them a chance of survival.

* * *

"Let's move!" shouted Kelly.

His helmet dome was folded back, being safe in the oxygen supplied tunnels. He could only hope that the enemy had not identified their access point to the surface, but he doubted they would have such luck. His people were exhausted and mentally hammered, but the supply drop was driving them on to give everything they had.

The Commander had already outlaid a plan for the food and ammunition to be divided between three key safe zones underground. They were all at least a mile from the drop zone. The few underground vehicles built to haul military and scientific resources throughout the tunnels were proving to be invaluable.

Since the invasion had begun, Kelly had done little but lose ground and friends. The supply drop had given him more than just hope. It had been intended to boost morale as much as provide genuine help, but it was much appreciated. He'd already been briefed on the necessity of immediate feedback on their new hardware. He knew they were being used as a test bed for the American military, but it was nothing he would complain about.

The crews sat atop the haulage trailers, many on the boxes of supplies. They smiled and slapped each other's backs. They were celebrating a victory. In any other situation Kelly would have talked them down, made them put it all into perspective. Today however, it was the only glimmer of hope that existed for them all.

* * *

"We've got incoming!" shouted Lieutenant Green.

The officer peered down over the rooftop at the APCs being loaded below.

"Shit! Get rolling, now!" Jones ordered.

The second vehicle was loaded as best it could be, but the third was still empty. He looked over to a sergeant who was next to him.

"Tell these two to get rolling and back within the perimeter, we'll follow ASAP!"

The Sergeant stared back with a gaunt expression. Jones had just volunteered for them to take the brunt of an attack for the good of the defending forces. He knew it was the right decision, but that didn't make it suck any less.

"Yes, Sir!"

The cannons of the heavy tanks bellowed around their position as the two vehicles began to roll, their heavy tracks ripping apart the civilian streets. Jones waved back the third and last APC. Gunfire erupted on the rooftop as his men began to engage the attackers, he knew it was a dire situation, but he had a task to do. Every fibre of his body told him to join his men in the fight, but the sooner they were loaded, the sooner they'd be out of there.

The driver was nervous and rushed, missing the Captain's command to stop. The huge steel beast smashed into the building. Bricks and motors tumbled down onto the soldiers below, crashing on their helmets. Fortunately, re-enforced armoury walls supported the structure.

"What the fuck!"

"Forget it, Sergeant, just get this shit loaded!"

Jones rushed to the crates of cannon rounds for the big guns and hauled them up with all his strength. His body was aching in every place, sweat dripped down his armour, adrenaline was the only thing keeping him going.

"Load! Load faster!"

The fire above was chaotic and desperate. The Captain knew that they'd been hit by a substantial wave of the enemy, but he would not return to the other survivors with anything less than what he had intended.

"That's it, Captain!"

Jones swung his rifle around to his front taking it in

both hands. He ran out of the building and to a corner of the structure to peer round at the unfolding battle. As he did so a huge energy pulse hit the heavy tank just twenty metres down the street. The blinding light soared through the thick armour and struck the ammunition store, sending it into a ball of flames. Black smoke bellowed from the wreck creating a smoke screen between them and the enemy.

Looking up to the ledge of the rooftop, he couldn't see any of his men but could hear their weapons still firing. He cupped his hands about his mouth and shouted at the top of his voice.

"Evac! Now! Go, go, go!"

He had no way to communicate with the other two tanks and he wouldn't risk any of his men to do so. He had to rely on the fact that they were observing the situation through their rear-mounted cameras. He signalled with his hands for them to pull back, hoping somebody was watching. Without wasting anymore time he turned back to the loaded APC, his men were already climbing aboard.

Green and the others from the roof slid down the ladders on the side of the building, desperately trying to escape the ferocious onslaught. There were less soldiers returning than had been sent up, but Jones knew that it was a waste of time to ask after them.

"Get onto the vehicle!"

The soldiers on top of the tracked APC hauled their

comrades aboard. There were now just seventy men left in his company. As many as possible were piling aboard the final APC, though only thirty were able to fit at a squeeze.

"Get this junk moving!" he shouted.

The APC lurched forward, leaving the Captain and more than half of his men behind. He turned to look back, praying that the others had gotten his message. They could hear tracks rolling, but they were muffled through the continuous gunfire and explosions around them. Out of the smoke the first vehicle appeared.

Several scorch marks were burnt into the armour plating. The tank stopped briefly to allow many of the men to climb aboard. Seconds later the second heavy tank burst through the thick black smoke. It barely resembled the first anymore. The turret was completely missing, blown off from a huge energy pulse weapon. Smoke bellowed from the engine block and the turret ring was still smouldering.

The driver's hatch was half destroyed and they could make out the bloody face of the distraught woman who sat at the helm. However wounded she was, she was still fighting. The men looked at the sight in disbelief. The destruction to the heaviest tanks in deployment made them all feel more mortal than ever before.

"Get on!" Jones ordered.

The last of the para company climbed aboard the scarred vehicle. There was nothing left of the two turret crew other than a trace of blood where they'd been ripped out along with the main gun turret. Through the gaping hole they could see that the hull gunner had been killed instantly by an energy pulse blasting right through his body armour and to the seat behind him. He lay slumped on the controls.

The driver was all who remained in the vehicle. Her helmet was off and blood poured from a head wound, she looked back for just a moment to see the soldiers clamber aboard.

Jones gave her the thumbs up and a nod, not just to confirm they were ready to move, but in appreciation and respect. The vehicle lurched forward with a creek. Pushing the vehicle to the limit of what it could still manage it would survive no more than a kilometre or two. Jones looked around at his comrades who had the grimmest of expressions about their faces.

The friends that they had lost were a tragic and earth shattering strike to the morale of the troops. But more so than that, they were coming to the realisation that they stood almost no chance of leaving Brest alive. The only relief was that they were giving hundreds of thousands of civilians the opportunity to escape.

Jones looked down at his hands. The gloves he wore were cut and blood seeped through from where debris had struck him. His armour was covered in a thick layer of dust from the destruction of the buildings all around him. His mouth was dry from the lack of water and smoke filled air.

As the vehicle stormed up the ruined street, Charlie looked back at the site they had left. He could see the bodies of two soldiers they had been forced to leave behind. The scene was peaceful again, the same horrible quiet that follows every bloody battle. Smoke still bellowed from the tank they'd lost. Turning a bend in the road he lost sight of the weapons depot and the carnage surrounding it.

Wanting nothing more than to forget everything he'd just seen, Charlie already knew that he never would, not for however many hours or days he had left to live. They had done everything that was asked of them, but it was at such a fearful cost.

It was not long before they reached friendly lines. The buildings around the perimeter were lined with troops from the French Armoured Corps. They watched, horrified at the sight of the smashed vehicle that they rode atop. Dozens of British troops were intermingled with the French soldiers, the few who from Jones' division which had managed to reach the city. They had fled there for safety.

The smoking wreck of the tank came to a halt in the crossroads where Girard and his command centre were setup. The APCs were already being raided for everything they had. The British troops leapt off the vehicle as Girard and Chandra closed in. Jones climbed to the front of the vehicle and knelt down beside the wrecked driver's hatch. The woman at the controls looked up at him with a haunted expression on her blood-strewn face.

"Captain Jones. Thanks for saving our arses, Sergeant."

He offered his hand to the injured driver. She first looked stunned, but then grasped his bloodied hand. Jones hauled her out of her seat quicker than expected. She was far lighter than he thought, shorter than any among them and close to half his weight.

"Captain! Good to see you made it back!" Chandra shouted.

"Major, we're a tank down, we lost plenty of soldiers out there, and whatever hit us will be coming down that road shortly!"

He helped the driver down from the vehicle, jumping down beside her. Girard noticed at the stricken driver with horror. He couldn't find any words to say to her. Chandra looked down at her body armour, just able to make out her name under the dirt and blood.

"Sergeant Dubois, get yourself to the aid station."

The bedraggled tank driver nodded. She could not bring herself to speak or to salute her superiors. She staggered off as commanded, still badly shaken over the loss of her crew. Jones turned back to his Major. He could feel that she was rapidly heading into same disillusioned state as the driver. Chandra was lost for words as she looked over his bloody and filthy armour.

"Captain, well done! You've kept us in to the fight. I must get these supplies moving, they are desperately needed!"

Jones nodded to the French Colonel as he rushed off to organise the distribution of the ammunition they'd brought back at such a high cost.

"Jones, you are to get back on the southern perimeter. We need every soldier in the fight," Chandra ordered quietly.

Charlie wondered if this new hell would ever be over. He supposed that death would be the only end in sight. He nodded before turning to his men and barking his orders. They glared at him in despair, not half recovered from the beating they'd just received.

* * *

Commander Kelly sat in what had become their operational headquarters. Computers had been hurriedly set up in a haphazard fashion with as much equipment as they could scavenge as time went by. Lewis sat at his makeshift comms desk. He barely knew what to do, having so little of the equipment and resources he'd been trained for and become so accustomed.

"Have you patched into the library feed yet?"

"Yes, Sir, we can now send messages directly from my station. It's a hardwired connection though, meaning this is the only terminal which can be used," replied Lewis.

"Understood, good work."

Kelly turned to look at the people at his command. Many of his surviving NCOs and officers lay about the room. Few conversations took place. The excitement of receiving help from Earth had already died down. Back was the grim realisation of the harrowing lives they now lived.

"Listen up! Everyone!" he shouted.

They all turned to him, wanting nothing more than to be told that everything was going to be okay. They hung onto the Commander's every word, praying he would bring them to victory or safety.

"The time for skulking around and scavenging what we can is going to stop. We can no longer scurry around, avoiding the trouble above our heads. We were sent new weapons for two reasons. One, to give us a fighting chance, and two, as front line testing for the U.S. military! We have an important task on our hands. We serve not just to fight for our own lives, but to help those who have done so for us!"

Kelly knew that many of his people still loathed the Earth based forces for leaving them in their time of need. Slowly they were beginning to understand that there had been no other option, but many still needed convincing.

"We have been given a second chance, and I fully intend to take it! It's time to take the fight to the enemy! I want twenty volunteers. I am leading the first party out to hunt those bastards down and see what these new babies can do!"

He held up one of automatic grenade launchers that Major Taylor had so recently tested back on Earth.

There was no instant cheer or hive of excitement. But people began to stand as the information was digested. The very idea of seeking out the fearsome enemy was still a horror to them all, but they were keen to get some payback.

"I'll go!" shouted Martinez.

Kelly didn't want to put both himself and his second in command in harm's way, but it was vital to lift the morale of his people. Within seconds others around the room began to stand and volunteer. They could all feel the fear of the enemy seep away as the excitement exploded among the soldiers. They began to cheer Kelly's name. He lifted his hand signalling them to pipe down.

"Martinez! Select a team and get them armed, I want a fifty-fifty split between rifles and these launchers! The rest of you, get the rations and ammunition distributed, you know what to do!"

Kelly slipped the sling of the launcher he was carrying over his shoulder and packed ammunition into the pouches in his armour. He only took the armoured suit off to sleep now. The burden of its extra weight was never welcome for prolonged periods, but it had become an essential part of his life.

The room burst into activity as everyone went about their tasks. The Commander had already carefully outlined plans for distribution and rationing, it was vital to both their survival and defence. Lewis looked up at him from his desk. He was the only person in the room with nothing to do.

"What do you want me to do, Commander?"

"Sit right here. We can still reach you through the hard lines, right?"

"Yes, Sir, but there are very few of them about anymore. I have people installing more throughout our underground facilities, but above ground, you'll barely find more than one or two per square kilometre."

"Okay, good work. I'll need you here for an immediate report to General White on our return."

"Yes, Sir."

The comms officer looked concerned. He was uneasy about two of the command staff heading off for combat.

"Lewis, you're in charge till we get back, stay sharp!"

"Sir!"

Kelly now had twenty grenades stuffed into his body armour. He pulled his weapon around his body and looked at it intently, making sense of it all. Within a second he'd found the chamber release switch. The front half of the weapon levered forward, allowing access to the revolving magazine. He loaded in a full eight shells from the box on the desk before slamming the weapon shut.

Turning back to Martinez, he could see that the team had already been selected and were busy loading up for the mission. The group was a mix of MDF and UEN soldiers. Previously they had treated each other with animosity and dissent. The MDF hated the UEN for being deployed on their colony and their eternal arrogance. The United Earth Nations troops had disdain for the MDF as being only a militia force. These feelings had melted away as they had quickly accepted each other as brothers in this new war.

"Let's not forget that we still face an enemy that we do not fully understand. We have likely not seen everything they have at their disposal yet, nor have we tried these new weapons. I want an even spread of rifles and launchers at all times. The launchers are all loaded with armour piercing rounds."

"Sir? Aren't we going to breach the compound with hardware like this?" asked Doyle.

"It's a concern, yes. However, at this point we have no choice but to upgun to whatever level we have to. Earth forces will also be using a high explosive shell, but for obvious reasons have not supplied those to us."

The soldiers pawed over the new launchers, not having handled such powerful personal weapons before.

"We honestly don't know how these will do against the Mechs. Choose your targets carefully and use your ammunition wisely. Everyone happy?"

The troops nodded. They were excited and scared in equal measure.

"Make sure you all have your air tanks and masks, a breach isn't ideal but we have to be prepared for it. We are heading half a kilometre north where we will enter the colony below the Metro gym."

Kelly watched as they loaded the last of their kit. It felt more like they were preparing for a hunt than a battle. Perhaps that notion was what kept their morale up, it was not something Kelly wished to compromise.

"Let's move!"

He led the way down a broad tunnel. They weaved in and out of countless people who were going about their business. The previous day had seen their new underground homes as a miserable place where the survivors of the colony lay about with little to do but grieve. Now every one had a job to do and it was forcing them to move on.

Kelly knew that the food supplies delivered to them would only last a week for the masses of survivors living underground, but it was a vital first step.

"Why the gym?" asked Martinez.

"We need to keep varying our entry points onto the surface to not present a pattern to the enemy. I picked it randomly as we have not previously used the access point there. The truth is that all we need to do is find some of those bastards and that won't be hard once we reach the surface."

Martinez knew all too well how widespread the enemy Mechs were. Fifteen minutes later they reached the two ladders that led up to the surface building. Climbing in full gear was no fun for any of them, not least for Kelly. He wished he'd kept in better shape, but it was to late to worry about that now.

They lifted the hatches above which opened up into a dark storage basement for the highly successful and up market gym. Kelly panted as he hauled himself into the room and rested on one knee for a moment, trying to hide his fatigue. After a few seconds he lifted the Mappad hung around his neck. Nothing showed on his scanner. He turned and looked to see the last of the troops climbing in.

He moved forward to the head of the column. Their military training had taught them to work in smaller teams and with greater spacing, but this new enemy had changed their strategy massively. When meeting them they needed maximum firepower at all times. The group of twenty-one kept close and alert as he led them up to the atrium of the fitness centre.

Just after arriving at the ground floor of the building Kelly got a reading on the Mappad device. He lifted his arm and signalled that a target was showing at ten o'clock. They all tensed and lifted their weapons ready. The huge glass walls dividing the gym to the walkway had been blown out in a previous fight.

Kelly signalled for them to hold their fire. They needed to know the effectiveness of the new weapons before unleashing a volley of fire. The men at the front knelt down, so that they could all have a clear line of sight at the opening just twenty metres ahead. They waiting silently as they could hear the heavy footsteps of the lumbering armoured Mech stomping towards them.

As he held the new launcher firmly at his shoulder, Kelly could feel his pulse racing and his heart pounding in his chest. A week before his wife had been warning him of the risk of a heart attack with all the stress he faced at his age. Now she was anxiously waiting in the make shift dormitory blocks as he fought on the front line.

Then it appeared, the ugly metal monster. It turned quickly as it caught sight of the soldiers. Before it could raise its huge energy weapon the Commander fired a single round. The large projectile hit the Mech just off centre of what would be the chest armour of a human. Landing like the punch of a heavyweight boxer, the enemy soldier stumbled back a step before catching its balance.

Kelly could see that the impact had hurt the alien, but it was far from dead. It quickly regained its composure and tried to lift its weapon again to target them. He didn't wait a second longer, quickly firing off two more shells. Each hit the creature square centre in its mass. The metal suit went limp as whatever was inside collapsed onto the broken glass with a crash. The soldiers stared at their fallen enemy.

"Holy shit," said Martinez.

Kelly turned to his number two with a smile. Finally they had a chance.

CHAPTER NINE

"General White! Report is in from Commander Kelly!" shouted Taylor.

He blurted out his words before he'd even got through the door of the Command Centre. The Generals immediately turned towards him. Any other time they would have disciplined him for his rudeness, but they were all more anxious to hear what he had to say than to how he told them.

"Speak, Major."

"At twenty metres, a single round hurt the Mechs bad, second and third finished it immediately!"

The Major had a broad grin on his face. He wasn't just satisfied that he had been right about the weapons, but that it would be enough to get them distributed and put into action right away.

"That's damn fine news, Major, good work! However, I

must tell you that I have already ordered the release of all stores to be allocated to combat troops and a further mass scale production to commence immediately."

"Sir? I thought you were waiting on the combat report?"

"For final confirmation, Major, yes. In all honesty, we didn't have time to wait for it, and we have all come to rely on you in these past days."

The Major gasped, realising how much responsibility lay on his shoulders.

"The United States will no longer stay out of the conflict in Europe, but our location and our allies, are best served by a direct attack on the enemy. We are about to mount the greatest assault that has been seen in generations!"

"General, the South American Union is willing to commit five thousand troops, as well as ships and aircraft to carry them," said liaison Flores.

"I have been informed that my government will match that commitment," said the Canadian envoy, Commander Brown.

"Thank you, then we have a great task ahead of us. We have been planning such an operation for days now. The Air Force has been carrying out almost continuous strikes against the western edge of Tartaros. Our job now is to organise a ground assault."

"How big are we talking here, General?" asked Taylor.

"Twenty thousand men will be deployed by a combination of air and sea following the last aerial bombardment."

"How much damage is the Air Force actually doing?" General Smith asked.

"They're having an effect, that's for certain. Breaches have opened up all along the monstrosity. Their casualties are high, but they're getting the job done. Ground forces will enter through these breaches, or blow their own where necessary."

"What kind of resistance are we expecting?" General Richards asked.

"Honestly we don't know. The enemy is powerful and in great numbers, that's for certain."

"We are throwing twenty thousand men into an unknown situation?" shouted Smith.

General White looked at the man with a pained expression. He was sick of dealing with the indecisiveness of many of his senior officers.

"The fact remains that this is going to be an unknown enemy in an unknown situation for a long time. Till we either get the upper hand and some real understanding, or humanity is wiped off his planet!"

"Major Taylor! Give us your opinion!" General Richards ordered.

"The Major is not authorised to deal with command decisions!" shouted Smith.

"I want to hear the Major out. So far he has been the one constant in this time of uncertainty," said Richards.

Taylor looked to General Richards. He had plenty to say on the situation but also knew how far he was stepping over the line by doing so. White looked at him, glad that Richards had requested his opinion. White had every confidence in the Major, but doubted the others would take him seriously in command decisions. Finally one of his peers had pushed the Major in the direction he wanted. White nodded to the Major to continue.

"Europe is getting a beating. North Africa is having it worse. We have all but lost the Moon colony, its surviving inhabitants hiding from the enemy. Safe in the Americas, not one of you can imagine the unrelenting horror that the world is facing. Way I see it, we either weigh in and fight alongside the rest of the human race, or we wait out our turn to be whipped."

"That's a grim picture you paint, Major," said Richards.

Taylor pushed his chair back and stood up with a sigh. His leg joints were aching from sitting around for so long, he was not at all used to life at a desk. He walked down to the end of the table where the huge display screen showed the conflict of the world.

"Look at this, all of you. It's not a map. It's a document of our losses as a species. We have to join the fight. Our options are to attempt to join the forces in Europe, which are quite frankly a mess. Or, we can open a second front. Hit back at the enemy. Right now, Europe needs us. But in the coming weeks and months, we'll need them just as much."

Richards nodded, he hated the planned operation just as much as before, but he was beginning to accept the Major's words. "If this is the only way, then so be it. But God help us all if it fails."

"Thank you, Major," said White.

Taylor went back around the desk, carefully studying their faces as he did. He knew that he would have to fight in the planned operation, just as the Generals knew, it was the overriding factor in their support of his outline of the situation. He took his seat as General White took a deep breath and continued on in a calm voice.

"There it is. We are making the best of a crappy situation, the plans have been drawn up. Major Taylor, report back to your battalion to prepare. I want marching orders sent within the next fifteen minutes to all operational commanders. Let's get this moving!"

The Major stood and saluted to take his leave as the others continued to begin the process of amassing the resources to make the assault a reality. Taylor had no idea when they intended to carry out the mission, it was above his station. He did however know that he would be able to count in hours the time before they deployed.

The sun was already going down as he reached his battalion drill square. Trucks were lining the previously clear training zone. They were at urgent deployment status. Two men of his company stood guard outside the building with his office, many more patrolled in every direction. The men saluted as he wearily stepped through into the hallway to be greeted by Lieutenant Suarez.

"What's the word, Major?"

Taylor didn't respond, he only signalled for the Lieutenant to follow him into the officers' mess. He opened the door to find it remarkably empty considering it served the entire battalion's staff. Captain Friday was sat alone and staring at a datapad. He leapt to his feet as he saw the Major enter, but he didn't ask the inevitable.

"Sit down, Captain."

The two officers took a seat beside the other.

"You know that I am bound by oath to not divulge any information that was shared in command. All I can do is repeat what you already know. Be ready, be vigilant. Deployment is imminent."

Friday nodded, but Lieutenant Suarez tried to probe further. Taylor lifted his tired head and put the officer in his place.

"You've done your time today. Major, get some rest," said Friday.

Taylor nodded in agreement and gratitude to the Captain.

"Have you handed out the new weapons yet?"

"No, Sir, they still remain top secret."

"Alright, I want the company formed up at 0700 hours on the square. Have the hardware ready for an introduction and issue."

"Yes, Sir."

Taylor stood up and strolled out of the room. He thought he would go right back on duty and to work, he had never appreciated quite how tiring it was to sit at a desk with the responsibility of the top commanders.

The Major barely remembered walking back to his quarters or even opening the door. Entering his apartment he sat down on the sofa to relax for just a moment. Within seconds he dropped into a deep sleep, still wearing his uniform and gun.

Hours later, Mitch's watch alarm rang violently, snapping him out of a deep sleep. For a moment he was disorientated, not even remembering having got to the sofa or falling asleep. He reached over to his watch and clicked the alarm off. It was set for 0600 hours every morning, unless he'd turned it off the night before.

Cupping his hands around his face he stretched the skin below his eyes downwards with his fingers, trying to wake himself up. His face was rough with stubble from the lack of shaving in two days. Running a hand over his shaven head he suddenly remembered the events of the previous day. He felt like crap, like he would after a solid day of heavy drinking. In an hour he would greet his company with new equipment and likely lead them into combat soon after. He knew that he had to clean himself up, even if it was the last thing he felt like doing.

He took off his gun and stripped his clothing off, throwing it down the laundry chute. Mitch stood in his shower, dazed as the water beat down on him. He could feel his state subsiding as the fresh water cleansed his skin and finally made him wake up. He stepped out of the shower, being hit once again by the morning heat.

Air conditioning was a luxury that nobody on base was afforded. General White felt that every man should be conditioned to the heat to enable them to operate effectively in such conditions. He moved up to his mirror wiping off the condensation. Taking his electric shaver, he removed all the stubble and hair within seconds. He went over to his wardrobe and pulled out a freshly cleaned and pressed set of combats, quickly putting them on.

For a moment he felt like a new man. Having gotten almost ten hours sleep and now finally awake, he had shaken off the fatigue of the previous days. Finally he felt ready to go forward with confidence and pride. He strapped on his pistol and strode out the door. Despite not being told when they would deploy, he knew it would be that day. The Generals had been given enough time to prepare and General White was raring to go.

Taylor was rested, smart and more determined than ever. He strolled confidently to the drill square, where earlier he'd ordered his men to form up. He smiled as the square came into sight. Friday knew the Major well and had formed up the company fifteen minutes early. He called them to attention as Taylor approached.

"Stand easy!" Taylor shouted.

He paced up and down the lines inspecting the troops. He passed Sergeant Parker who gave him a playful grin that went unnoticed to all but him. It brought a warmth to his heart as he remembered who he was dealing with. D Company were not just the troops he commanded, but his family, his friends, everything he loved.

"We will shortly be receiving our marching orders! Most of you have first hand experience of the enemy, and I am sure you have brought the others up to speed. The enemy is strong. They are powerful, intimidating and alien. Don't be fooled! They can be killed, they will be killed!"

"Oorah!" they cried.

"The most obvious deficiency in our last engagement was found in the lack of effectiveness of our weapons against the thick armour of the Mechs. It's time for that to be resolved!"

The Major stepped up to three crates which Captain Friday had laid out ready for him in front of the troops. He lifted off the lids of each and pulled out the first weapon, holding it up for them all to see.

"This is the M97 automatic grenade launcher. You will have all seen it in the manuals. They have long been out of service due to the disarmament programmes around the world. They have already been tested against our enemy and have proven to be extremely successful. The armour piercing ammunition is effective up to around fifty metres, maybe a little more."

The Major could see that several of the troops were looking uneasy at the range element. All of their primary armaments were effective up to a minimum of five hundred metres.

"It's close range work for sure, but you'll appreciate them in the field, trust me. We have about enough for one in four men. High explosive ammunition may be effective at longer ranges but we simply have no proof of that yet. You will be supplied both for now."

He put the launcher back down into the box it had come from, reaching for the next.

"Ortiz and Campbell, next weapon is for you!"

Pulling out a hulking sniper rifle, he held it aloft with both hands. If stood against a man it would be the same height as the tallest of any marine stood on the parade ground. A monstrous magazine fed the weapon from behind the trigger in a Bullpup configuration.

"These anti-materiel rifles were built to punch through armour at a fair distance. They won't touch the heavy tanks we now use and therefore likely not the enemy's either. However, the armour penetration is equal to the M97s, up to four hundred metres at least. We have five of these, so I want you to select three others with high marksmanship ratings to join you."

The company snipers looked at the vast weapons in

astonishment, being over twice the size of what they had been accustomed to.

"Lastly, the ARMALs have proven to be useful on the battlefield but they don't pack enough punch. You will still carry them, as much is in short supply. However, we have got twenty of these Aardvark devices. They are really just a bigger, meaner version of the ARMAL and will be distributed one per section. Any questions?"

"Sir, are the rest of the Corps receiving this hardware?" shouted Sergeant Silva.

"Yes, Sergeant, but not in this number. We have been given priority due to our previous experience and the nature of our unit. General White has been releasing all stores to personnel and has already put urgent operational order requests in for fresh production."

Taylor could see the uncertainty on their faces. Most of them had seen what a struggle it was against small numbers of the creatures, open combat was a frightful thought.

"The reality is we do not have the equipment or technology we could do with to fight this war, but that has not stopped great nations from gaining victories throughout history. We are the best there is and we will give it our best shot. Any man or woman who doesn't wish to fight should never have joined the Marine Corps. A great General once said, 'Americans love to fight. All real Americans love the sting of battle'. He also said 'A good plan violently executed now is better than a perfect plan executed next week'.

Taylor paced up and down the line, desperately trying to think of words to reassure his troops though he already knew he could rely on them.

"Fact remains, we will likely never have the best weapons in this war. Nor the best tanks, the best planes, the best anything. What we have is the raw determination to survive and give them hell. We will prevail, we will because the fate of our entire race depends on us!"

The Major felt the datapad device in his pocket vibrate, the sign of an urgent message from command. He pulled it out as the marines before him anxiously waited to hear what news he was receiving. Taylor looked back up with an expression of relief. All realised that the time for waiting was over.

"This is it, gentleman! Captain Friday, distribute the new weapons and ammunition! Full battle order and aboard the trucks in ten minutes!"

* * *

Captain Jones' rifle ran dry and he dipped back down behind the wreck of a vehicle he'd been using for cover to reload his weapon. Sergeant Dubois ran up and ducked into position beside him. The driver's wounds had been cleaned but her forehead and cheek showed deep cuts that had been sealed with spray seal. She carried a rifle she'd clearly picked up from a fallen soldier and stuffed magazines into her filthy body armour.

For a moment the Captain thought about telling her to fall back and leave them to it. It was completely against all regulations to have a wounded member of the vehicle crew joining front line infantry. Then it came to him, the realisation that the modern regulations no longer counted for much in this war. They needed every hand on deck and every weapon in action. He appreciated her courage as much as her efforts. He nodded in gratitude as she rose above the wreckage and opened fire.

As Charlie slammed in the next magazine to his rifle, he looked back at the bodies of four of his men strewn across the road behind their positions. They were just a handful of the casualties in the bloody struggle to defend the tiny patch of the city centre they still held onto. The Captain had been given command of a company that morning, but now he was almost down to a platoon size once more.

"We're getting annihilated, Sir!" shouted Saunders.

Jones thought for a minute. He looked up to the buildings around them. His troops continued to give the enemy everything they had as the buildings were collapsing all around them. He peered back over the barricades to see ten of the Mechs advancing down the street towards them.

"Why don't they just nuke us?"

Jones looked to his batman who was stricken but still fighting back with a bitter hatred of the enemy. Then it struck the Captain. The enemy surely had the firepower to vaporise large areas just as they did.

"They want our planet, and without us on it, Private. Think what damage our nukes do. They don't just want to kill us, they want our lands!"

"Whatever, Sir, we need to get the fuck out of here!"

Looking back down the street he could see that Major Chandra was dashing towards him with two of her marines at her side. A huge section of wall from a nearby building smashed down and crushed one of her men, narrowly missing her before she reached the Captain.

"Jones, we just got a Dart message from Rennes! Evac is in ten, we are to get to the rooftops immediately!"

The Dart system was antiquated technology that was only kept for emergency measures. It fired a targeted message module with pinpoint accuracy, using the theory of carrier pigeons used centuries before. It was a system for when all other technology failed.

"Got that, Captain? The boats won't hang around, if you're not there in ten then you're on your own!" she shouted.

The Captain nodded with a reserved sigh. He had given up hope of surviving the siege. He was still dubious as to whether they would make it out alive, but at least it was something to lift the troops' spirits. He looked to the men around him, knowing he needed runners to relay the message.

"Saunders, you take the buildings to the east, Hughes to the west. Relay this message, evac in ten, immediate withdrawal!"

The men quickly ran off into the now derelict buildings from where the troops continued fighting from. Jones leapt up and carried on laying down fire on the Mechs approaching their position. He looked back to the few troops left along the barricade.

"Come on! Give it to them!" he balled.

The runners didn't spare a moment in recovering their comrades from the buildings. Any fatigue was immediately forgotten as the news of their rescue spread. The remaining troops poured out, some helping their wounded comrades who had fought on through injury.

"That's it, fall back!"

Jones took to his feet and started to move back with the rest of the troops. The barricade and wrecked vehicles provided cover for their retreat, at least until the enemy reached them. He counted the troops as they rushed back towards the centre of the crossroads. He counted thirty-eight, including Dubois.

It was doubtful that anymore than a handful were at the aid station. Jones' fear that he had lost close to three platoons out of four was a reality he was hoping not to have to face. Reaching the square he found Major Chandra and Colonel Girard ushering troops into the two tallest buildings either side of the road.

The French armour had been entirely abandoned and the troops funnelled into the buildings in a desperate hope of escaping the fate of many of their friends. Chandra looked at Jones' bedraggled company jogging up the street, many being assisted.

"This all that survived?" she shouted.

Charlie nodded, he could not bring himself to say it. She was as distraught as him, but quickly snapped out of it.

"Alright, Captain, get your arse up top!"

Running through into the building that was a high class fifty-storey office complex, he could see troops pouring into the twelve elevators and many more queuing to use them.

"The wounded stay for the elevators, anybody still on their own two feet takes the stairs!" he ordered.

Jones smashed through the doors of the stairs and didn't even break stride, leaping onto the first steps. He was already breathing heavily. It was in this moment that he appreciated the gruelling training regime they'd endured on a regular basis. All hated long runs in full armour, but it had readied them for this very moment. Not only were they running from the enemy, but also they all knew they had limited time.

Finally smashing through the rooftop doors, Jones'

exhausted men were greeted by the sight of countless aircraft with troops piling aboard. An explosion erupted in the sky as an enemy ship zoomed by and blasted a troop carrier out of the sky as it lifted off. Friendly fighters rocketed by with guns blazing.

Seeing a craft land not far to their side, Jones immediately rushed towards it, despite how dead his legs felt.

"Run!" he shouted.

They clambered aboard the vessel and sat helplessly hoping that they would make it out alive. From the windows in the side of the transport they saw the alien and human fighters battling it out. They saw at least ten friendlies drop out of the sky as the pilots placed themselves between the enemy and the transports.

The ship lifted off and immediately went to full throttle, darting across the sky. Seconds later they were away from it all. Gone were the deafening sounds of battle and the death and destruction all around. Now they sat in silence, hearing nothing but the faint drone of the engines. Not one of them could think of a word to say, they merely stared at each other in a combination of despair and relief.

* * *

Once again the Major sat looking at the troops which lined the copter they were travelling aboard. Gone were the cheerful jokes and larks that had echoed through the vessel during their training mission just days before. Their training had prepared them for a full-scale war, but none of them ever expected to face it.

Their briefing had been short and rather vague compared to most training briefs. It was clear they were on a mission full of uncertainty. The Canadian and SAU forces had already embarked via sea in the middle of the night. The marine forces attacked via air in a combined operation.

Taylor knew that this mission was a test bed for future operations. The attack was not intended to gain ground, but simply to occupy it for a short time, causing as much damage as possible to the enemy and giving relief to the war in France.

Without any idea of objectives or layout of the enemy island now known as Tartaros, the human troops were being piled in to cause as much trouble as they could. The expectation was to take and hold the western beachhead for no more than a day, killing as many of the enemy as possible and setting explosives on the way out. The Major didn't like the lack of intelligence and knowledge about their target, but knew that they had no choice but to act.

Standing up, he walked along the fuselage of the ship and up to the cockpit. He looked out between the two pilots at the monstrous alien island before them. All around them were hundreds of aircraft. Fighters, bombers and transports. Up ahead they could just make out the shapes of the sea-based craft approaching the enemy. Tracer and energy pulses flew across the sky up head as their fighters engaged the enemy.

"ETA two minutes, Sir!" shouted the pilot.

"Thank you, Lieutenant!"

The enemy's jamming technology had already stopped all communication via radio. Taylor missed his usual flight crew. It had become tradition to fly with Rains and Perez, but he knew that they were playing just as important a role. He went back to his men.

"This is it! Remember, you were born for this! This is our chance to take the fight to them!"

The troops stood in readiness. Moments later the familiar approach began with the raising of the nose and reverse thrust. The doors opened and the Major leapt out first, followed immediately by his companions. The boosters kicked in on his suit as he approached the alien landing zone. For a moment his heart almost stopped as he could make out a Mech at the very point he was descending. Then he saw the wisp of smoke rising from its suit and realised it lay dead on the floor.

As he landed next to the fallen enemy the Major was immediately looking in all directions. Marines were landing on the deck all around him. They were dropping through the vast holes that had been blown into the roof of the structure. The large room was five metres high and mostly empty, though the roof sections that had fallen in provided substantial cover.

"Major, check this out," said Suarez.

He pushed his way through the men to where the body of the fallen enemy lay on its back. The bombing runs must have struck the alien as its armoured suit was smashed and ripped apart. For the first time they gained a glimpse of the creature beneath the suit. The creature's head was visible where the top of the armour had been blown off.

The head was of human size, though taller and slightly narrower. The skin was dark blue. There were features similar to a human, such as two eyes, but the nose was almost flat to the face. The structure had been disfigured by the blast and light blue blood was strewn over the skin and armour.

"That's disgusting," said Kwori.

"I'm sure it would have said the same thing about you, Private," replied Taylor.

"Yeah, well this is our planet not theirs."

"It's a fair point. We've seen enough, let's move."

They could hear a constant drone as boots hit the metal floor for more than a kilometre in either direction as the battle continued to rage in the sky. Before they could make another step, a door lifted open at the far end of the room.

"Mechs!" shouted Baker.

The marines turned, rushing to open fire as energy pulses began to fly at them. The two enemies didn't even get through the doorway as they were riddled with fire from much of the company. They breathed a sigh of relief for a moment. Seconds later a larger door opened further along the same wall, revealing Mechs in a ten -wide line and as deep as they could see.

"Take cover!" shouted Taylor.

Light pulses killed six of the marines before they could even reach the debris in which to hide. The room erupted into an ear splitting hail of gunfire as the troops began to fire back. Rockets and grenades smashed into the armoured aliens and blew many apart, but more followed. Taylor saw several more of his marines get hit as they returned fire.

"Keep firing!"

His voice was drowned out by the gunfire all around him, but it was the only thing he could think to say. His jaw dropped as he saw the wall in front of them fold and open, revealing lines of Mechs. Behind him the marines continued to drop in and join the fight. They had made no headway yet and were already in a meat grinder.

"My God!"

"Get the high explosive rounds in! Aardvarks, everything!"

Seconds later the room erupted into a dazzle of flashes and bursts of light as explosions broke out around the enemy attackers. Another ten marines fell and as many of the Mechs were blown apart. As Taylor watched the onslaught a pulse from an enemy weapon smashed past his head into the cover he was using, knocking him to the floor unconscious.

An hour later the Major woke up in a scattered pile of bodies. His hearing was buzzing and his eyesight blurry. He stretched out his hand and pushed to lift himself up. As his vision cleared he could make out at least forty dead marines, he'd been left for dead. Scrambling to his feet, he shook his head, trying to wake himself up.

He stood alone in the vast room. Dozens of Mechs lay dead and destroyed before his position. For a moment he thought he had been left alone on the alien hulk. His hearing began to recover and he could make out the familiar sound of rifles firing. It was a relief to know that his forces were still in the vicinity. He attempted to walk but swayed slightly, still disorientated and off balance.

Making his way through the dead marines and aliens, he headed for the gunfire. Far into the distance he could see as many as a hundred marines fighting, but taking a bend there was action far closer. Down a vast corridor he could see his own company frantically defending a wall of piled dead Mechs. He could just make out Captain Friday's voice bellowing orders to the men.

Between him and the troops lay five more dead marines. It had been a bloody struggle to make just a few hundred metres into Tartaros. He lifted his rifle and saw that the magazine was nearly empty. He changed it as he staggered forward and began to regain his composure. As he closed in on his company's position he could see that it led to an opening in a huge room the size of a football stadium. Two other companies were dug in and fighting hundreds of Mechs advancing from the far end.

Captain Friday turned abruptly as he caught sight of movement behind him. Realising that it was the Major he ran up to Taylor hauling him down into the defences.

"We thought you were a goner, Major!"

"Give me an update, Captain!"

"It's as it looks, Sir! You must have been out for some time. We're hitting them hard but they just keep coming at us!"

"Any command signals yet?"

"No, Sir!"

"This is fucked, Captain!"

"Yes, Sir!

"Have the engineers set the charges!"

"Already done, Major!"

Taylor nodded in appreciation. Friday always knew when to anticipate orders, but never overstepped his command. Over the sound of the gunfire and explosions they could just make out the piercing sound of a siren coming from their original location.

"That's it, Captain, signal for full retreat!"

Having their communications jammed meant that they had reverted to using audio signals as commands. The

Air Force had launched audio beacons into the breaches just moments before to signal the retreat. Taylor knew it would be a tough battle, but nothing like the onslaught he was seeing.

"That's it! Fall back!"

The marines looked in surprise at hearing their leader's voice once more. Seconds later they got to their feet and rushed with every energy to escape the bloodthirsty scene. Taylor took a few paces back into the entrance of the corridor and watched as the survivors of the company rushed past him.

He turned to look back at the defences just the second as an energy pulse smashed into Parker's flank slamming her to the ground. Her armour was smouldering from the heat and she was lifeless.

"Eli!" he shouted.

Taylor rushed back into the open ground to her body.

"Major! Come on!" shouted Friday.

The Captain's words were utterly ignored as Taylor reached his fallen Sergeant and the only woman he'd truly loved. He threw his rifle around to his back and hauled her onto his shoulder. He had no idea if she was even alive but he would not risk leaving her even if there was no chance of her being saved.

Light pulses smashed into the wall behind the Major as Captain Friday returned fire with his rifle, doing his best to cover him. The shock of seeing Eleanor hit had sent such adrenaline pulsing through Mitch's body that he had found a second wind. He stormed across the floor and into the corridor.

The entire company ran with all the energy they could muster. They reached the room where they had originally breached and found the Air Force pilots had smashed new holes in the hull allowing them to land at their level. They clambered aboard gratefully. Taylor laid Parker down in the seat next to him. He was oblivious to anything as he checked to see if she was breathing.

Captain Friday was the last aboard and barked at the pilot to get in the air the second he had a foot in the door. The pilot lifted off and immediately spun the craft around speeding off westerly. Captain Friday watched as many of the other ships desperately tried to escape, many were destroyed in the process.

Pulling out his datapad, Taylor quickly checked a few details before running up to the cockpit.

"Glad you made it, Major!" shouted the pilot.

"Lieutenant, you have new orders, I want you to take us to these co-ordinates!"

He thrust the datapad forward for the pilot to see, but the man looked confused and uneasy.

"Sir, I have orders to evac you immediately back to base."

"I have a Sergeant in there who is dying, there's a British destroyer north of here that you can reach in half the time!"

"Sir, I have my orders."

Taylor snatched his pistol from its holster and placed it up against the pilot's head. He froze in shock.

"Lieutenant, this is not optional!"

Captain Friday stepped up also in shock.

"Sir, what are you doing?"

"Stay out of this, Friday!"

The Captain knew better than to interfere with Mitch. His superior had also become his friend over the years. No matter how crazy an idea was, he'd learnt to trust Taylor under any circumstances.

"Lieutenant, get us there, now!"

"Alright, alright!"

It was a relatively short journey to the British destroyer HMS Battleaxe. Everyone aboard knew that Taylor was directly contravening the orders of their command, but not one of them had the heart to stop him. The other craft carrying his company were quick to follow suit, having every confidence in their leader even without knowing his intentions.

The surviving marines of D Company dropped onto the deck of the carrier. Their pilots refused to land with them, returning as ordered to base. Of the one hundred and nine of the company who had got off the enemy island, they carried only eight wounded. They had left seventy-one marines dead in the hellish alien hulk. 'Leave no man behind' was an ideal they could no longer afford to adhere to.

The British Navy and Marine crew were shocked to see their American counterparts, but eager to assist. Some rushed to help the few wounded, though most stood in shock at the distressed state in which the soldiers were. Taylor carried Parker immediately to the medical bay as Captain Friday reported to the ship's Captain who came out to greet them. The Royal Naval Captain gasped upon news that they were a company upon seeing their numbers.

Taylor burst into the doctor's medical bay. The Doctor reeled at the sight of the fully armoured and armed marine crashing unto his impeccably clean and kept room.

"Doc, this marine needs your help right now!"

CHAPTER TEN

Charlie looked out through the windows at the French scenery below. He'd become well accustomed to recognising it from the air. He could see enemy Mechs and tanks rolling down the roads. They were approaching the base at Rennes, though they were not slowing or dropping altitude. He watched as the base came into sight. It was nearly empty, with the last few vehicles rolling out and heading east.

Getting up out of his seat the Captain strode forward to the pilot's cockpit, as much to talk to them as to see easterly.

"Thought we were heading for Rennes?"

"No, Sir! The enemy are closing in fast. They are closing in on Le Mans from the south as well. All forces are being directed to Paris!"

"My, God, it's come to this already?"

"Yes, Sir."

Jones staggered back to his seat, he could not believe what he was hearing. Now he was beginning to understand why they had been left to defend Brest. The situation had been far worse than they had realised. Their defence likely delayed the enemy by many hours, perhaps even a day.

The transports that had made it out of Brest finally put down in a public park not far from the centre of Paris. They were not greeted by a crowd or even ground crews. As Jones jumped out he saw that Brigadier Dupont and Commander Phillips were waiting for them with no more than a dozen soldiers. Buses were waiting to take the wounded to a nearby hospital. The survivors of Brest left the craft but had little idea what to do with themselves until finally the Brigadier climbed onto the back of a small truck and got onto a loudhailer.

"Welcome back, all of you! I would like to personally extend my gratitude to all of you that have made it, as well as the many more who were not so lucky. A lot was asked of you over the last few days, and I am sorry for your losses. However, I cannot be sorry for the task you did. You have saved the lives of hundreds of thousands of people!"

No one responded to the Brigadier, they were too stunned and traumatised from their experiences.

"As much as I would wish you all to have adequate rest and leave, we are in a state of war. The enemy approaches

Paris in vast numbers. We will need your courage and strength once again in the coming days. For now I ask that you rest easy here. I will see to it that everything you need is brought to you. Please rest and await further orders, that's all."

Saunders turned to his Captain, angry at the speech they had just heard.

"Wow, we go through hell and that's the thanks we get!"

"If you wanted thanks you shouldn't have joined the army, we did what we had to."

Jones was relieved to see trucks arrive with food and water. There was little that could help them feel better at that moment, but that was it.

"Captain! Come with me!" shouted Chandra.

The Captain sighed, he was just about to sit down. He stretched his body as he walked, aching from the days of fighting. He walked up to a meeting of the surviving officers with Commander Phillips, the Brigadier was already leaving the scene on his personal truck.

"Any ideas on numbers?" asked Phillips.

"Not exactly. However, I estimate about three thousand troops entered Brest, I think little more than three hundred made it out."

"Christ, we can't afford those losses!"

"Yes, Sir. How is the rest of the division doing?"

Most fell back after the defeat at the coast. We fought running battles all the way to Rennes where we finally made some headway. Casualties average maybe thirty percent of the division, a damn sight better off than your para boys."

"Sir, I think we have enough to amalgamate into a single company."

The Commander shook his head.

"Do it! Paris is becoming the number one priority. Infantry and Armoured Divisions are setting up on the west and southern perimeter. We've got maybe a day until they hit us. Emergency shelters are en route, I suggest you all get some kip."

* * *

"Major?" asked the Doc.

Taylor was hunched in a chair outside the medical room with his head in his hands. He shot up in hope of hearing some good news.

"She's alive and stable for now."

"But?"

"But she needs surgery, work I cannot do here. We're en route to Portsmouth right now, she can get the care she needs there."

"Will she last that long?"

"We're on emergency conditions right now and therefore travelling at maximum velocity to our destination to assist the rest of the Fleet, her condition should remain stable until we reach the port."

Taylor nodded and sighed in relief.

"I am not promising anything, Major. She'd sustained massive injuries, but she has a chance."

"Thank you."

He stood up and continued up through the decks until he reached the open air. Many of his marines sat about the deck with their kit strewn about. The Navy crew had never seen the deck in such a state of disarray, but nobody had the heart to tell them to sort it out. Taylor walked up to a railing overlooking the waves as they crashed below. They were indeed travelling at an immense speed for the size of vessel.

"How is she?" asked Friday.

Taylor turned to see the Captain stroll up to him and rest against the railing bulkhead.

"She's got a chance once we get to Portsmouth."

The General's gonna have your ass for this, you know that don't you?"

"Under normal conditions, yes. Look around us. The rules have gone out the window. White needs me and needs us, he'll just have to accept it."

"What about the assault on Tartaros? It wasn't exactly all we hoped for."

"No, but it was something. We had to take action no matter what."

"What do you think the brass will do next?"

Taylor lowered his head and stared out at the waves.

He'd been so focused and single minded after Parker had fallen that he'd given no further thought to the situation.

"They've accepted that we have to keep up the fight. If attacking Tartaros directly isn't realistic, they'll look to fighting on the ground. My guess is they'll be organising combat in North Africa and Spain as we speak."

"And us?"

"I have nothing left to help the brass with. We are no more experienced than thousands of others now. We'll fight wherever we are needed. Once we reach Portsmouth I intend to request that we join the EUA forces in France."

Friday nodded. He knew what the Major was saying was that he wanted to help their friends, just as he had saved Parker. He was aware that there was far more than a professional relationship between Parker and the Major, but also it was best not to interfere. The Major was letting his emotions drive him. Many would say it made him unpredictable, but Friday knew it made him a good leader.

"Major! I have General White on the line for you!" shouted the ship's Captain.

"Looks like the devil has found you."

Taylor smiled at Friday's sharp wit. On any other occasion he would dread the call from the General after disobeying orders. However, after everything he had given, he feared nothing. He stepped up to the bridge and pulled on the headset as he sat down.

"Taylor here."

"Major, I know why you did what you did. I have also been informed of what you and your men sacrificed today. You care about those under your command like family. I can respect that. How is your company?"

"Down, but not out, Sir."

"Good to hear, because I have a new task for you."

"Sir?"

"The EUA are rallying around Paris and making a stand there. They're calling in all the help they can get. We are working on a new strategy for a ground attack. However, seeing as you're already there, I want you to rally with British para battalion under Major Chandra."

"Chandra? What happened to the senior officers there?"

"Dead, as are most of the battalion as I understand it. You are to join them under her command."

"Sir, I have a marine in critical condition here in need of urgent attention."

"I am aware of the situation, Major. I have already dispatched transports from our UK bases to get her to the facilities she needs and to get you to Paris. They'll arrive within the hour."

"Sir, I fully apologise for breaching orders."

"Understood, Major. We all do what we have to do. The attack on Tartaros was brutal, but we gave as good as we got, it has to have hit them where it hurts. You have your orders, good luck and give them hell."

"Yes, Sir."

Taylor pulled off the headset with a wide grin on his face. He was glad to be wrong about the General. White had given him hope and a chance to be exactly where he needed to be. The Captain tried to speak to him but the words fell on deaf ears as he dashed off the bridge. He leapt down the ladders to the deck where his marines were waiting. There morale was as much affected by his mood as anything else. He could already see the fire in their eyes grow as he approached them with his shoulders held high once more.

"D Company! Gather round!"

The troops eagerly assembled to hear the news. Combat deployment was a given, it was no longer to be feared. More than anything, they wanted payback against the brutal enemy that had mauled them so heavily just hours before.

"Today we struck at the enemy on their own turf for the first time! We never expected to hold ground. Yes, we hit heavier resistance than expected, but we did it. The brass is already planning their next attack. Right now our biggest concern is that our allies in Europe are taking a beating!"

"Was it worth it, Sir?" asked Price.

Taylor looked up at the faces of his marines, still shocked at the losses of their friends.

"As marines we chose to put ourselves in harm's way. In

Europe the alien bastards are gunning down civilians and the EUA forces are doing everything they can do to fight back. We fight and die so civilians don't have to. There are people's families being murdered every minute."

"What are we going to do about it, Sir?" asked Silva.

"Paris is has become the stronghold of France. General White has ordered us to head there and lend a hand. We are to rendezvous with the 2nd Parachute Battalion and do what we can."

"What is their status?" asked Friday.

"From what I hear they have had it a lot worse than us. We are to combine with them under the command of Major Chandra, who I suspect will be a Colonel by the time we arrive."

Sighs rang out across the marines at the idea of anyone having a worse time of it than their experiences.

"That'll be all, gentleman. Wheels up in under an hour, be ready!"

* * *

It was late at night when Taylor's company set foot in the public park where they had been deployed. Pop-up tents had already been erected ready for them to rest out the night. In the distance they could hear the rumble of tanks and the construction of defences as fresh troops continued to toil away.

There was no sign of the British parachute battalion, though he imagined that after the mauling they'd received they were catching up on some much needed rest. The camp guards showed them to their tents and they gratefully lay to rest for the night.

Taylor woke naturally as the sun beat down on his tent. The light and heat were enough to awake him from even the deepest sleep. Having no further equipment and clothing he went out of his tent with stubble on his face and the previous day's blood and grime. He was surprised to see that the British troops were already formed up for inspection as his marines were scrambling out of bed. Their discipline never ceased to amaze him.

"Stand easy!"

Taylor recognised the voice of Charlie Jones as he strode along the line of his troops. The Major ambled over to the Captain, still feeling the weariness of the previous day. The Captain turned to face the Major with a grin.

"I see the yanks have finally decided to join us!"

Taylor smiled as he shook hands with the Captain. Jones' face was rough with cuts and bruising. They looked at their distressed and dirty uniforms, realising that they must look as bad as each other.

"Glad to see you made it, Captain, I hear you had a rough time of it."

"And yet here we are, still on our feet!"

He looked back to his men and shouted for them to fall

out. He beckoned for the Major to follow him a few steps out of the hearing of his troops.

"Mitch. I put on a brave face for them, but it's been frightful. I was made acting company commander in Brest, my company can now only amass one platoon, which is what I have had to amalgamate them into."

"Christ, how about the rest of the battalion?"

"It's now at company strength. How many marines did you bring with you?"

"I have one hundred and one, all that is still fit for duty in my company."

"Glad to have you with us, but we could do with a hell of a lot more."

"Agreed."

Major Chandra approached with a smile. They had always had a good working relationship with Taylor's unit.

"Major, glad to have you here. However, there is no time for pleasantries. The enemy's an hour or two from our perimeter. I am merging your company with ours. Henceforth we shall be known as the 2nd Inter-Allied Battalion. Full gear and ready to march in ten."

Taylor nodded and gave a quick salute before running back to his marines who were still rising from their beds.

"Everyone up! Fall in! Full gear!"

He rushed back into his tent and pulled on his body armour that was still covered in dust and debris. Starting the day in filthy clothing and without a wash was never something the Major would wish on anybody, but needs must. He stepped out from his tent to find the platoon assembling.

"Where's Baker?" he asked.

Suarez looked at him with a gaunt expression, conveying everything in his eyes.

"He was killed shortly after we thought we had lost you, Sir," answered Friday.

In his frenzy to save Parker, Mitch had failed to investigate the survivors to see who was left. As he looked down the lines of his company he began to notice the many gaps. Dozens of men that he'd known, each by name, most for several years.

"Very well."

He looked out to the troops who went silent and waited. He didn't call them to attention not seeing the necessity for formality. He looked to Captain Friday.

"Are we ready for action, Captain?"

"Sir, we could use some ammo, otherwise we're good to go."

"It's already in hand!" shouted Chandra.

Mitch turned to see the woman striding towards them. "Major."

"It's Colonel today, I have been given a field promotion in order to take official command of our battalion, even if it is at less than half strength. Your report on urgent weapon requirements made quite an impact Major. The

EUA has already been distributed its stocks. We can't spare any weapons for you, but we can give you ammo for what you have."

"Much appreciated, Colonel."

"When you are assembled, you will find the ammunition stores near our camp."

Thirty minutes later the combined Marine and Para battalion was on the march with a full load. There was not a single vehicle spare to ferry them to the front line. Every transport vehicle that could be mustered in France was either taking troops to Paris or civilians away from it. However it was only thirty minutes on foot to the defensive lines.

The troops looked in horror at the largest deployment they had seen in their lives. Divisions of armour lined the perimeter, many having been put into hull down position. Lines of self-propelled artillery and batteries were assembled along their route. ABD, Automatic Barrier Defence structures, had been set up in almost continuous lines in the streets and crossroads. Paris had become a fortress.

The 2nd Inter-Allied Battalion took up position in a well-prepared defensive position that the fresh infantry units had prepared for them in the night. Deep trenches with tank traps a hundred metres ahead. There were so many troops deployed to the city that their space allocation was so small they were shoulder to shoulder. Clambering into the trenches they could not help but think of the photos of the gruesome combat of the First World War.

"Back into the fire," said Friday.

Taylor grinned. "True, but at least this time we have some real numbers."

"Incoming!"

They didn't know where the call came from but it was enough to make all the troops duck down into the trenches. A huge energy pulse soared overhead and crashed into a building behind them. Glass and concrete burst out onto the street below. They looked up at the damage but another five similar devices landed in quick succession around their position. Dirt and tarmac fragments were thrown up and over them as they hunkered down.

"What the fuck is that!" shouted Kwori.

"I'd say their artillery has arrived!" Jones shouted.

The soldier looked at him with a grim expression.

"You thought we'd seen everything?"

"I'd hoped so, Sir!"

Alien craft zoomed over their heads as further fire rained down all around them. Their dug in positions gave them cover from the worst of it, but the outer limits of the city where they were positioned were quickly being reduced to rubble.

"Where's the fucking Air Force when you need them!" Suarez called out.

Taylor looked over to Chandra who was already barking

orders into a handset. Anticipating the radio jamming which always accompanied the enemy, spindles of hard lines had been run out to all positions. It was a stone age way of operating for the troops, but a vast improvement over the blackout they'd previously experienced.

Lifting himself slightly above the trench, the Major looked out west from where the main enemy forces were advancing. The sky was filled with hundreds of the enemy craft using their familiar chameleon camouflage technology. In the skies above he heard the rattling of cannons and snapped his head around to see wedge formations of friendly fighters soaring towards the enemy gunning down the first of their targets.

The men in the trenches let out a cry of excitement as they saw the aerial combat unfold. Artillery fire continued to rain down on their position, but the ground attack from the aircraft had all but stopped. The lines of artillery behind their defences began to fire in a deafening barrage against the enemy targets.

Looking over the edge of the trench, Taylor could not yet make out the enemy positions, though their artillery had certainly received enough information to begin their attack. He glanced over to Captain Jones who looked confident and ready for everything they were about to face. Taylor had heard of the British troops flirt with death, he wondered if anything could wither their resolve.

The sound of a plane dropping towards the earth at

high speed caused both of the men to look quickly to see a friendly fighter plunge into the road just twenty metres from them. They ducked down at the last moment as the plane erupted on impact and rumbled the ground beneath them. The battle in the skies raged for another thirty minutes as the artillery continued to rage thunder down upon either side.

Finally the enemy bombardment ceased. Far from the relief which some might expect, the troops knew it was the signal for a ground assault to begin. In the war torn skies above the fighters continued to battle it out. The humans were losing four fighters for every one of the enemy's, but they continued to slug it out.

An immense sound of tracks could be heard in the distance even over the drone of the battle overhead. Jones imagined the alien invaders had underestimated the resistance that the inhabitants of Earth would put up, but they were quickly upping their game. Up ahead they could see nothing but shops and housing blocks. The broad roads were completely empty. In the distance they could see the very first of the alien vehicles rolling towards them.

The artillery at their backs continued to roar. Taylor only hoped they'd brought enough ammunition to keep up the fight. Explosions littered the roadway leading to their position. They could just make out the sound of the enemy tanks as they came nearer to their defences.

"Nobody fires until they reach three hundred metres!

Choose your targets carefully!" shouted Chandra.

Either side of their position were heavy tanks dug in and adjusting their elevation in readiness. Seconds later the ground shook as the vehicles recoiled at the firing of their main guns. Of the first two shells, one landed short of the enemy column, the second hit but did not slow them down. An apartment block in the distance collapsed as a vast enemy tank ploughed through it, shortly followed by more at its flanks.

Now at only a thousand metres the enemy forces were expanding into a broad front. The guns of their tanks opened up and began pounding the human positions. An artillery battery behind the lines was vaporised by the first volley. Several men were hit in a nearby infantry trench, though most of the fire had little effect. The defensive positions were so far providing excellent cover.

The intensity of the fire increased as all guns came into range and the EUA armour opened up with everything it had. Ahead of their position were five tanks and a hundred Mechs approaching in a fearless fashion. The first bombardment smashed an enemy vehicle and it burst into flames and thick black smoke.

Three of the Mechs were tossed aside like ragdolls by a shell from the heavy tanks. One scrambled back to its feet but the other two were done for. The return fire smashed into their positions and badly damaged one of the tanks at their flank. Screams of pain rang out from the trench the other side of the crippled vehicle.

"Six hundred metres! Be ready!" shouted Taylor.

The Mechs opened fire with their huge handheld energy weapons. Light pulses soared above their heads as the troops peered over the positions at their unrelenting enemy. One of the rounds slammed into the helmet of one of Green's platoon, taking his head clean off.

"Four hundred! Ready!" barked Chandra.

The half strength battalion rested its weapons along the embankment of the trench that was dug into the tarmac and concrete of the road. Three of their troopers lay dead from the artillery and gunfire before they had yet managed to fire a round. The Aardvark launchers and anti-materiel rifles were carefully aimed and waiting for the go ahead. Every one of the troops was eager to rain down hell on their attackers.

"Fire!"

The trench erupted into a continuous volley of fire. Two rockets from the Aardvarks knocked one of the tanks out. The rifles and BRUNs were slowing the Mechs' progress but rarely finding the weak points they needed to cause injury. M97 launchers fired off high explosive rounds with relative inaccuracy igniting all around the alien positions. A few ignited near the feet of some of the Mechs, blowing their legs off and rendering them useless as they fell to the ground.

Taylor laid his rifle down, pulling the grenade launcher

from his back that he'd taken from one of the wounded on the British destroyer the day before. He fired off the high explosive rounds at the advancing Mechs. The first two hit the ground showering them with debris. The third struck one of the metal monsters dead in the chest and it exploded on impact. The beast was lifted off its feet and tumbled back in a twisted wreck.

Smiling at his efforts, Taylor was reminded of the grim reality of quite how little ammunition he had for the weapon compared to the growing number of enemy. Half of the enemy tanks in their sector had been knocked out, but their own armour was doing little better. The Mechs and surviving tanks continued to advance through the eternal rain of bullets and explosions.

"Get the ARMALs!" Jones ordered.

The men pulled the handheld devices off their backs and readied them. They knew how effective they could be at close range. The enemy were now just two hundred metres away. A pulse of energy smashed into the trench beside the Captain and Saunders, and another two of his platoon were killed instantly. For a second he looked in despair at their bodies, but quickly took up the ARMAL launcher they had been preparing.

The Captain didn't have to give out any further commands. The men around him had already begun firing with the devices and everything else that they had to hand. As he armed the device he could see Major Taylor loading the AP rounds into his launcher. He nodded at his friend before taking aim. The ground the enemy had covered surprised him, it was far closer than he had anticipated.

Hoping to fire at one of the approaching tanks, Jones caught sight of a Mech turning quickly to fire at him. He snapped the weapon around and fired right at the beast. The round landed lower than expected, at the hips of the metal suit. The explosion caused the suit to scissor as if it was hinged, crumpling into a twisted mess.

The enemy tanks had reached the traps the EUA forces had hoped would stop them. However as they drew near, huge curved blades as broad as the vehicles themselves and slung low on the hulls began to spin. They met the traps with a deafening grinding as sparks flew in every direction. The vehicles were slowed, but were cutting their way quickly through the devices.

"Hit them now!" shouted Chandra.

Every soldier in the company with an ARMAL or Aardvark stood up and took aim with no regard for their own lives. They could only imagine the horrors they would face if the enemy armour got among them. The surviving crew of the crippled tank beside them continued to fire despite the smoke bellowing from its turret.

The company fired in a frenzy with everything they had. The tanks erupted with such heat that they could feel it inside the trenches. They watched as the Mechs began to step back. They continued firing but were in withdrawal.

The troops continued to fire and the snipers took down another two as they clambered out of range.

Jones climbed up on top of the tank with the least damage on their flank. He stood with no fear for his life. Taylor leapt up beside him with his launcher. He reloaded as he stepped up top, not wanting to be caught with it empty.

The two officers looked out across the width of the battlefront. Burning wrecks littered the battlefield along with hundreds of lifeless Mechs.

"Have you ever seen anything so pretty in your life?" asked Jones.

Taylor smiled. It was the first time in the war that they had seen the enemy retreat or be defeated in any number. The continuous losses they had faced made them all wonder if they would ever stop the alien hordes in their tracks. Taylor turned to see Chandra standing at the vehicle next to him.

"How does it look, Major?"

"Come and see for yourself, Colonel!"

He offered out his hand to hoist her up. She initially looked insulted at the sentiment. It was never made easy for a woman in the military, even less so for Chandra who operated in an elite unit. Taylor smiled in a way she could see was both being friendly as well as larking about. She smiled back and took his arm. Taylor hauled her up onto the vehicle where she could see the wonders before them.

For a moment she let herself revel in the victory they had achieved. Seeing the enemy crushed was the most heart warming experience since the war began. Then, as Jones and Taylor continued to gaze at the fruits of their labour, Chandra turned back to look at their own lines and felt a sickness in her stomach.

Tanks and artillery were in ruin and hundreds of soldiers lay dead or wounded across the lines. She could see similar devastation in the distance. The alien forces had attacked across a several kilometre-wide front. She estimated that thirty percent of the troops of the units she could see had been decimated. It was a brutal reminder of the losses in Brest, and a horrific insight in what was to come.

"We paid a high price for this small victory," she said.

Taylor and Jones turned to look at the grim sight. Their smiling faces were quickly muted as they looked at the carnage on their own side.

"I hope they are losing as much as us, because we can't keep this up forever."

"We have no choice, Colonel. This isn't a war of our choosing. They want our homes and we have nowhere to go, we fight or we die as a race," said Taylor.

"Our American friend if right, Colonel. No price is too high, for extinction is the only other option."

She nodded and turned to look back out towards the battlefield. She could just make out the last of the Mechs and vehicles retreating.

"They'll be back soon enough, and in greater number. No one likes taking a beating and they'll be eager to set the record straight."

"We'll be ready for them!"

"Captain, get on the line, we need ammunition and re-enforcements brought up immediately. I am guessing their next assault will be twice as strong as this one was. Also make sure we get plenty of water, and organise the wounded to be moved back!"

"Yes, Sir."

He leapt from the tank to carry out his tasks. They had made the city of Paris a fortress, and in doing so they all realised what a siege it was about to become. The first of the re-enforcement detachments were already clambering over the rubble on the road from the centre of the city. They poured into the trenches as the wounded and dead were pulled out, more lambs to the slaughter.

"Colonel!" shouted Lieutenant Green.

She turned to see the man pointing at a fresh wing of enemy aircraft heading for their position.

"Into the trenches! Take cover!" she screamed.

She leapt with Mitch from the tank landing hard in the trench below, crumpling to the floor. Seconds later the first of the strafing runs began and bricks and mortar peppered their positions. They watched as half a section of re-enforcements were annihilated on the road east before they could reach any solid cover.

The strafing run was just the beginning. Moments later they were overhead and bomb-like objects dropped all around them. The defences burst into light as continual explosions erupted. The troops could do nothing but huddle in their trenches and hope for the best. The remaining tanks tried to counter the aircraft with their secondary mounted anti-aircraft weapons. They knocked out a couple of the alien vessels, but it had little effect.

Taylor could see Chandra shouting orders, but couldn't hear a single word despite her being only a metre away. The ground shook and rumbled continuously as if hit by an earthquake. A nearby bomb struck Price, blinding him instantly and leaving his face cut and mangled, he was alive but no good to anyone. Taylor saw him moving and wailing but couldn't hear his screams over the deafening noise.

The bombing run raged for fifteen minutes until friendly aircraft arrived to once more do battle. However it was too late, the alien planes were already returning west and the EUA fighters were forced to turn back in fear of being over hostile lands.

Taylor and Chandra stood up to survey the damage. Both tanks were now utterly destroyed and another eight men were dead in their trench, as well as many more wounded. The Colonel remembered dispatching Captain Jones just moments before the attack had begun, she could only pray she hadn't sent him to his death. Seconds after the distressing thought the Captain appeared from behind one of the burning wrecks to report in.

He stopped and looked around at their trench for a moment. Blood trailed up his armour but it seemed it wasn't his. He looked back to the Colonel dumbfounded.

"Sir, you had it light here, I suggest you take a look."

Chandra clambered back onto the tank she'd been on before the bombing began. The vehicle was smouldering and she could feel the heat through her boots. Looking along the line of defences she gasped at the carnage. There were gaping holes in their defences where entire trenches had been left as ragged craters. Most of the armour on the front line was blown apart or still burning.

In the distance came the frightful sound she had been dreading. Tank tracks in vast numbers were rolling towards their positions. Still a couple of kilometres off but in great numbers, she doubted they had more than fifteen minutes before all hell broke loose. Jumping off the vehicle once more she strode to the wired phone in their trench and ripped the handset from its cradle.

"This is Colonel Chandra, get me Commander Phillips!"

"This is Phillips."

"Sir, we're in deep shit here! We've got heavy casualties. Our armour is mostly gone. Enemy is approaching in substantial numbers, I do not believe we can survive another assault!"

"Understood, Colonel. Brigadier Dupont is receiving

the same reports across the line. I am ordering you to withdraw immediately! A defensive line is being setup along the banks of the Seine. Fall back and take up positions there. Good luck, Colonel."

The Commander cut off the transmission, but Chandra had already heard everything she needed to know. She turned to look at the troops in the trench. A few were helping others to patch over minor wounds, though most were awaiting her orders.

"Immediate fall back to the Seine! Carry all wounded! Leave the dead! Let's move!"

The troops hated leaving their fallen comrades, but were also relieved to be leaving the site of such slaughter. Their previous victory had been bittersweet after the mauling they had just received. As they got to their feet they could see that the other infantry regiments and surviving vehicle crews were already pouring down the main roads.

Seeing the front line armies in full retreat was a morale destroying experience. It was half an hour before they reached the river bridges and streamed over them. Two fresh EUA divisions had deployed along the banks of the Seine and erected even greater defences than they previously had.

The clean and fresh soldiers stared in silence at the battle fatigued and battered combat troops as they rushed back behind the new line of defences. Not even the best-trained and equipped armies of the world had faced such a voracious foe. The new line of defences had thick concrete barriers inset either side of the trenches creating blast defences. Heavy armour was lined up all along the roads facing across the river.

Officers from the signals units directed the combined company to their new area just twenty metres off from the entrance to a wide road bridge. They had been allocated a line of four-storey buildings built as defences for the bridges a hundred years before. The thick walls and strong structures were a welcome sight to the troops defending the vital area of the river.

Taylor and Jones were quick to deploy their troops to every defensive position that they could. Even the wounded no longer able to carry their own bodyweight were propped up with plenty of ammunition. Within five minutes the troops were ready and taking a much needed rest.

The two officers found their Colonel on a roof looking out west from where the enemy was approaching. Charlie and Mitch walked up to her as she panned across the city. Smoke plumes still rose from the battleground they had fought on that morning.

"They've stopped," said Chandra.

"You sure?" asked Taylor.

"Listen."

The three officers stared into the distance just listening for anything. Troops continued to march on the roads behind them, but the front was quiet.

"Do you think they've had enough?" she asked.

"Not a chance. Think what we would do if the enemy had retreated to greater defences. They are pausing to amass their forces before a grand assault. This could be it, this next battle could decide the fate of one of the greatest cities in the world," said Taylor.

CHAPTER ELEVEN

The troops of the 2nd Inter-Allied Battalion had laid about in their defences for over an hour. Ammunition supplies were brought up and troops continued to pour in from the west. Their communications were working as normal, though the signals staff were still working hard at installing wired connections in readiness.

Taylor, Jones and Chandra sat in a corner of the rooftop defences of their building. It was the calm before the storm which all of them had now experienced more times than they had ever wished. They had re-supplied and were as ready as they could be. Now the only thing to do was wait. Despite the communications lines working, they had received little contact from Headquarters.

"Jones tells me a Sergeant that you're very close to is in a critical condition in England," said Chandra.

The Major looked over to Jones with a humbled

expression. Both the British officers understood that he had more than a professional relationship with Parker, but didn't mention it.

"How is she?" she asked.

"Last word the Commander was able to get said she was still in surgery."

"Then she's in a better place than us," said Jones.

"Really?"

"She's got a solid chance of survival, better than our odds."

The Major smiled, he appreciated the Captain's humour in an attempt to settle his grief. The huge advertising display boards on the buildings opposite flickered and caught their attention. The EUA logo appeared on all the screens that had survived the earlier bombing raids. The three officers and the few troops sitting about the rooftop got to their feet and walked to the far side of the building.

They didn't know what to expect as the huge building-width displays flickered and then faded to a conference room with the EUA logo and lines of the countries' flags. A podium stood in the centre of the image. It was the familiar set up from which all key speeches and announcements were made by the heads of the EU.

The scene was vacant of any sign of life or movement. Suddenly a woman stepped up behind the podium. She was dressed in a smart suit and looked confident and calm. She turned to the camera looking directly into the lens.

"This message is for all EUA forces and allies thereof. I have with me the representatives of all thirty-one states. We come to you live from London where the President of France and his Majesty the King of the Great Britain and the Commonwealth have travelled to address you personally. Please welcome President Andre Francois."

The woman left the podium as all the troops at the defences were fixated on the screens. None were ever particularly interested in what politicians had to say, but in this time of need, they clung onto any news they could get.

"Greetings to all of you. To the men and women of the European Union Army, and the many troops who have joined the fight. I want to extend my gratitude to every one of you that is fighting for the freedom and survival of not just our country, but the entire world. I am well aware that time is not on our side and will therefore be brief. You honour us all with your courage. Thank you, and good luck. Now may I present to you, his Majesty King Richard, the Twelfth."

The French President moved aside and the King stepped up to the podium. In his fifties, and a former soldier himself, the graceful and confident royal wore his blazing red tunic and full regalia.

"Ladies and Gentleman. We have lost the west of France. We have lost Spain. North Africa has also fallen. We cannot lose Paris! I have just received word that four divisions are en route from Russia and its allies. Troops from the Middle East are already arriving in Italy and Yugoslavia. Help is on the way, you have my word! All that matters now is that we all accept that failure is not an option. To fail is to condemn our families, friends, comrades and children to death. The world is looking to you, and you will have our eternal gratitude for the sacrifices you make. Good luck to all of you."

The King lifted his arm in a salute that was returned by all who were watching the screens, before they cut off and went to black.

"Guess there wasn't much else to say," said Taylor.

"What else do you say when faced with global destruction?" asked Jones.

Chandra stopped and listened as a signal came in through her commlink.

"Enemy's on the move, all troops take up positions and..."

The signal cut off in the same way that they had become familiar with. Chandra turned to notify the others in her command but was beaten to it by the opening barrage from the gun batteries positioned behind the lines.

"I guess they're on the way then!" shouted Taylor.

"Affirmative, Major. Enemy forces are incoming! Captain, get on the hard line and find out what commands were being given before we were jammed!"

She glanced at the other troops on the rooftop who

were looking around as if not sure what to do.

"Everybody get downstairs and into position!"

As the Colonel turned to make her way off the roof the first of the enemy artillery fire smashed into their building. The second energy burst landed close to her tossing her off her feet and across the floor. She crashed into the opposite wall.

Taylor regained composure a few seconds later and found himself resting face first on the hard floor. He clambered to his feet and could see Jones already attending to the Colonel. One of his men lay dead, his body almost torn in two. Taylor staggered over to the officers. Chandra was breathing but roughly, her leg was mangled and bleeding.

"We have to get off this rooftop!" he shouted.

Jones looked to the Major and quickly back to his superior. She was badly wounded, but he knew that she would likely not survive if they stayed up there any longer. She winced in pain as he took hold of her, her body was badly battered. Throwing her left arm over his shoulder he lifted her with both arms.

Another energy pulse crashed at the opposite end of their position and sent fragments of the structure bursting into the air. The only relief was in seeing that the bunker itself remained structurally solid against the onslaught of the enemy's barrage. Jones carried her quickly down the stairs, leaving Taylor to slam the thick old doors shut behind them.

Taylor rushed to where Chandra had been put down, the lights flickering all around them as each blast that landed nearby rumbled through the structure. Jones had already run down to the next floor to find their field medic.

"Great timing, hey, Major?"

"You're still breathing, Colonel, there's a lot to be said for that these days."

She grinned, gritting her teeth as the pain wracked through her body. "I'll make it this time, but I am in no state to command."

"Colonel!"

"Once the blood flow is stopped I'll be at a window with a rifle, but the battalion is now yours, Major."

He nodded in acceptance. He had become accustomed to the responsibility of important missions, but none quite as vital as what they were now experiencing.

"This isn't the kind of promotion I ever planned for, Colonel."

"Nor here. All I ever wanted was promotion, now all I want is to see us survive this shit."

"Damn right!"

Jones rushed back into the room with the medic.

"The doc can handle it from here, you two need to get to your positions. Taylor now has command, give them hell!"

The two men stood up, saluting her with grim

expressions on their faces. The battle had barely begun and they were off to a bad start. They went to to the nearest window. The narrow firing slots ran along every wall of the structure and were protected by a wall that was over a metre thick. They couldn't yet see the enemy forces that were approaching, but the artillery and air combat raged all around.

There were no more orders to be given. They knew they had to hold their position at all costs. Taylor and Jones stood side by side, fixated on the view of the broad road up ahead that led to the bridge they were defending.

"Guess this isn't the way you imagined going out?" asked Taylor.

"No, but our ancestors have a long history of dying for their country in this land, we can at least keep with tradition," replied Jones.

Moments later they saw a rocket trail soar down the street as the infantry forces to their flank opened fire on the enemy that were still out of their line of sight. Taylor could feel the grimy sweat between his palm and the grip of the launcher in his hands. He looked back to see the crates of ammunition stacked up behind them. At least they could stay in the fight if they could just survive.

"Target!" shouted Jones.

Before they could even take aim the men on the floors below them had opened fire. The two enemy tanks which first came into sight were hit with a hail of crossfire from troops occupying both the river edge and the buildings behind. The tanks erupted into flames, but only came to a halt for a few seconds as the next vehicles shunted them aside and continued onwards. Mechs appeared at their flanks and were already laying down fire.

High explosive shells landed among the tightly compacted formations of the enemy and they were blown apart, many plunging into the river either side of the bridge. They could see a number of the armoured infantry scattering into the buildings opposite them.

"Keep an eye on those windows!" Taylor ordered.

He caught sight of the first Mech in a window just inside a tall old building. Firing instantly with his high explosive grenades the old windows shattered and the wall blasted through. Further Mechs poured into the hole in the cover of the building.

The gunfire was so voluminous that not a trooper among them could distinguish the sound of individual weapons firing. Light pulses smashed into the re-enforced building taking chunks out of its armour. A lucky shot burst through the firing slot down the line from Jones and took the head of one of his men clean off. He stopped for just a second staring at the scene before turning back and fighting on.

The windows through building the other side of the river lit up as the enemy took up more positions and began laying down fire on their bunker. Taylor ducked down to reload his launcher as Jones kept up the fight. Gunfire poured from all floors of their structure. They could hear mass footsteps on the stairways leading up to their floor and those below. Taylor locked his launcher shut and held it in readiness.

Taylor was suddenly elated by the sight of EUA forces bursting into the room.

"Colonel Chandra!"

An officer barked in a course Scottish accent.

She gestured over to Taylor as the Major stood up and went to greet the troops. The battle raged in the background as Mitch shook hands with the man.

"Major Douglas at your service, we're here to help."

"Major Taylor, I have taken command of the 2nd Inter-allied. The enemy have taken up positions in the buildings along the river and their tanks continue to try and get through on the bridges."

"Let's see if we can give you a hand, Major."

Douglas lifted his rifle and walked straight to the firing positions with Taylor and a number of his men. They opened up with a volley of fire from every weapon in their arsenal. Explosions erupted all along the building but they quickly recoiled at the deafening sound of a tank exploding on the bridge.

Quickly recovering they concentrated their fire on the lower building sections and the troops in the floors below quickly followed suit. Glass and brickwork smashed across the road in front of the building as it was hammered by rockets, grenades and machinegun fire. They could just hear the aged creak of the building as its foundations began to crumble. They watched in awe as the lower floor gave way and the five storeys above it came tumbling down, crushing the Mechs defending it.

Cheers rang out among the combined troops of the bunker and the infantry lines outside in the trenches. Taylor rushed along the line to look out at the gun ports looking down their side of the bridge. Medics were dragging away dozens of wounded from the trenches and many more lay dead. Looking up the river he could see that similar battles raged on every bridge as far as he could see.

The gun batteries of the enemy opened up once more, pounding the buildings behind them and the friendly artillery positions behind those. The bunker rocked on its foundations as several huge impacts struck the floor below them. Screams of the wounded echoed up the stairwells.

"Keep firing!" shouted Taylor.

He rushed to the frontal positions to see that fresh enemy troops were already marching over the dusty rubble that covered their comrades. As the dust settled over the ruins he could make out the countless tanks and Mechs approaching in the distance. He gasped at the sight of it before quickly lifting the launcher to his shoulder and firing a full load into the advancing troops. Kwori dashed up the stairs to reach the Major who turned to reload his weapon.

"Sir! We've got twenty dead on the next floor down, another fifteen below that, we're getting fucking killed here!"

"That's our job soldier!"

"We have to retreat, Sir!"

Taylor released his grip on the weapon and slapped the man across the face.

"Get yourself together, Private, and man the fuck up!"

The marine looked sheepish. They were all exhausted and astonished at the chaos and bloodshed all around them, but there was no choice but to fight on.

"Is Captain Friday still alive?" shouted Taylor.

"Yes, Sir!"

"Get back to him, you take up your weapon and you fight marine! No retreat!"

The Major loaded the last of a full load into his launcher and turned back to the fight to see artillery shells smashing the enemy positions, but as many flying overhead in their direction. Buildings either side of the river were being reduced to rubble. The bunker they defended was only still standing due to its excessively robust construction.

Enemy tanks drew into view that appeared much like Jones had seen previously on the beaches south of Brest, though they had vastly larger turrets and guns. They continued firing as they saw the gun of the nearest tank elevate to their height and fire. The wall just ten metres from Jones' position smashed inwards, punching a hole as tall as a man. The three soldiers there were thrown across the floor in a mangled mess. Taylor looked at the fearsome vehicles approaching.

"Take out those tanks!" he shouted.

The Aardvark launchers began to fire but it wasn't soon enough. A second shell smashed into the floor below, rocking the bunker and almost taking Mitch off his feet.

"Everything you've got on those tanks right now!" he barked.

He ran to the edge and opened fire with his launcher, firing repeatedly at the nearest tank. Over twenty-five grenades struck it and eleven Aardvark rockets before the turret was pierced and knocked out of its mountings, rendering it useless. Before they could target the next tank another two massive energy pulses smashed into their building. One of the shots smashed out a large section of their defensive wall and went through the roof, causing rubble to collapse and kill one soldier.

The troops immediately ran to the firing lines and continued to rain down fire on the remaining two tanks. Mech fire piled through the gaping holes in their structure but all fire was concentrated on the vehicles below. Seconds later the second tank erupted into flames. They turned their attentions to the third but it fired at their top floor. The blast expanded a previous hole and sent Taylor and Douglas sprawling across the floor.

"Take it out!" shouted Jones.

Taylor heard the immense explosion from the floor where he had been thrown. He got back up to see that Major Douglas' armour was smouldering from a broad chest wound. He shook his head in despair at the death all around him. He got up on one knee and looked around to see that there were more than twenty dead on his floor alone. Looking up to the defences he could see that Jones still fought on alongside a mixture of troops from all three units.

He staggered to his feet and up to the ammunition crates. Flicking open the launcher he loaded it once more and packed his webbing with as many spare rounds as he could get. Despite still carrying the rifle on his back, he knew what little it could do against this enemy. A light caught his attention from the corner of his eye as the battle raged on, it was the hard line comms. Stumbling over to it as he sealed the ammunition pockets on his vest, he picked up the handset.

"Bombing raid incoming on your position, fall back fifty metres from the river, over."

"Who is this?"

"Orders direct from Brigadier Dupont. Inform Colonel Chandra to fall back immediately, you have three minutes to haul arse, over."

Taylor threw down the handset and snapped his head around to look at the survivors who continued to fight at the walls.

"Fall back! Fall back! Now!"

The men initially looked at him with both shock and disbelief. It was the command they had hoped for from the beginning but never expected to receive. They had all prepared themselves to fight and die where they stood.

Taylor and Jones rushed to Chandra who was propped up at the end of one of the firing positions.

"What's going on, Major?" she shouted.

"Dupont has an airstrike incoming, we've got three minutes to get the hell out of this death trap!"

The two men got either side of the Colonel and wrapped her arms around their shoulders, taking the weight off her crippled leg.

"Everyone out now!" shouted Taylor.

There were few wounded in the bunker, most being killed outright by the onslaught of the enemy's heavy weapons. Friendly artillery continued to fly overhead and pound the enemy positions. They stormed down the stairwells of the bunker. Only half the soldiers who had entered the battered building had made it out alive. They rushed across the wide-open street towards the next line of buildings fifty metres back from the riverside.

Taylor shouted to the infantry in the trenches as they passed by. Some were already leaping out and following the troops fleeing back, others stayed and fought on. The hole-ridden bunker at their backs did them one last service, giving them cover as they fell back. They could already make out friendly troops that had taken up positions in the tall commercial buildings they were approaching.

Chandra squirmed in pain as the two officers hauled her. They were as surprised as she that she'd survived the explosion, but it was little relief in the ongoing battle. The occupying troops filled every window in sight with their weapons at the ready. One building had completely collapsed between two of the friendly positions, its rubble provided ample cover.

"There!" shouted Taylor.

"Damn right, I'd rather die fighting than be crushed when the next building comes down!" Jones added.

The survivors from the bunker swarmed into the ruins and immediately took up position looking back towards the bridge where they'd run from. Many of the troops in the trenches continued to fire at the advancing enemy with everything they had. The air was suddenly filled with the reverberating drone of a huge wing of heavy bombers.

Looking overhead, Taylor watched as a wall of fighters stormed across the sky with all guns blazing. Rocket trails filled the air as missiles soared towards the enemy aircraft. The fighters were cutting a path through at a great cost to make way for the bombers. Lights pulsed in the sky as ground weapons fired up against the mass of aircraft.

Their attention was quickly drawn ahead as an enemy tank had managed to gain a foothold on the bridge and brush aside the countless burning wrecks. It rolled on past the trenches as the troops had little left that could stop it.

"Tank!" shouted Jones.

The men in the buildings next to them had already opened up with their weapons but most of the gunfire and ARMAL devices were bouncing off its thick armour.

"Get the Aardvarks firing!" he shouted again.

Captain Friday ducked and weaved in between the rubble as the gunfire increased. The tank's three guns were firing relentlessly into the friendly position and blowing holes out of the building.

"Sir! Aardvark ammo is almost out! Grenades are getting low too!"

"Just keep firing!"

Trails from the rocket launchers slammed into the tank as it continued to roll towards them. The main gun lowered in readiness to fire at their position just as a volley of rockets slammed into it causing the vehicle to amble to a halt. Holes littered its armour and there were no signs of life. As they stared at the result of their work, they had failed to see what was happening overhead. Massive explosions erupted around the river instantly deafening them all.

The troops ducked down as stone and glass was projected hundreds of metres through the air and the ground shook. Taylor lifted his head just a little to look at the carnage up ahead. Bombs smashed the enemy positions in an almost continuous stream for as far and wide as his eye could see. The ear splitting onslaught was excruciating and many simply dropped their weapons and covered their ears.

For a solid five minutes the barrage continued and the wreckage of enemy vehicles and Mechs was scattered and blasted into thousands of pieces. Buildings collapsed all across the waterfront and beyond. The trench positions disappeared into a ball of smoke as the friendly positions there was utterly destroyed. The brave troops who had kept up the fight were all but a memory.

Some of the troops began to scream from the unrelenting assault all around them. Their mouths were wide and faces taut, bellowing with all their energy, though nobody could hear them. Finally the bombing came to an end. As Jones' hearing began to recover he realised how unsettling the new silence was. Smoke and dust clouds still filled the air.

"They've done it!" shouted Silva.

The troops now blended in with the rubble they occupied, dust and grit sticking to every spec of their clothing and armour. Taylor stood up to look out at the scene. The bunker they recently occupied had lost its two upper floors but was still standing defiantly. Over the other side of the water they could see that the streets had been flattened. Stacked rubble had all but covered the remaining wrecked vehicles.

The centre of the river bridge had finally collapsed. The Major sighed in relief. For a moment he thought they had won the fight, but his face quickly turned to a grimace as the sound of tracks began to roll in the distance. The men stared in terror across the rubble but were unable to make out any movement due to the thick cloud of dust.

None of them could believe that the enemy could have survived the onslaught in any great number, and yet, tanks were approaching. They looked once more at the bridge and were thankful that it had finally fallen. Through the dust cloud a few Mechs appeared. They were covered in dirt and filth so that they blended into the ruins just as the humans did. Seconds later the first tank burst into view.

"What are they doing?" asked Ortiz.

He lifted his huge anti-materiel rifle and slammed it down on what was left of a   pillar next to them. Lifting the stock to his shoulder he peered through the scope at the increasing number of enemy who were still six hundred metres away.

"What the fuck is that?"

"What is it?" Taylor shouted.

He yanked out the binoculars from his webbing lifting them to his eyes. The vehicle was taller and wider than anything they had seen but he couldn't make out any weapons on it. The monstrous tracked vehicle continued to roll towards the bridge, other more familiar vehicles following and Mechs were pouring towards the river.

"It's a bridging tank! Take cover and be ready!"

"Sir, we can't hold back another assault with armour, we have barely a heavy weapon among us," said Jones.

Taylor looked around in desperation. He prayed that the troops in the buildings alongside them still had rockets, though he knew it was too much to hope for. Huddling behind the massive piles of rubble and walls still standing, the survivors of the battalion had grim expressions. They knew that they were being asked to give up their lives to defend the city, but they still held on to the hope of victory even in the face of the dreaded alien armies.

Taylor knelt down beside Captain Jones. Friday was ten metres off to his side behind the remains of the front wall of the building. Chandra had perched herself against a section of fallen roof and held her rifle at the ready. The vehicle rolled right up to the surviving ledge of the bridge and came to an abrupt halt.

"Do not let them pass!" Taylor ordered.

The top unfolded and expanded outwards across to their side of the river. As it did so the body of the vehicle lowered as it spread out and locked into position forming a solid path over the river. The next enemy vehicle roared to life and began to trundle towards the newly formed bridge.

Then from behind their positions Taylor could hear a mechanical grinding noise that was becoming louder. As the enemy vehicle got onto the bridge it was hit by a huge shell that punctured its hull. It pulled to one side and collapsed into the river. Taylor turned to see a huge tank roll forwards from behind the building at their side, shortly followed by more.

Having never actually seen one, other than in pictures, the armoured behemoths were instantly recognisable as the T15 super heavy tanks. They rolled on without hesitation, firing as they moved. The first of the enemy vehicles erupted into clouds of smoke as Mechs were tossed aside by the immensely powerful guns.

"The Russians!" shouted Kwori.

The troops let out a hail of excitement and shouts as twelve of the huge vehicles rolled into position. One of the T15s was struck by an energy burst and rolled to a halt. The crew clambered out, the immense frontal armour saving their lives. A roar of battle cries rang out from the street where the tanks had come from and moments later troops poured out into the open. Hundreds of the Russian troops swarmed in to assist the armour.

Taylor and his men stood in their positions watching as the enemy were entirely blotted out of view by the surge of men and tanks. Cannons and machine guns fired in a brutal push towards the river. The 2nd Inter-Allied could only stand and marvel at the fearless courage of these men.

As they stood there, as surprised to see their allies as they were to still be alive, a vehicle rolled up. Commander

Phillips leapt off as the battle continued to rage.

"Major Taylor! Glad to see you made it!"

Mitch quickly saluted the man as he approached. Phillips stood and stared at the battered and bloodied troops. He could barely distinguish between the three different outfits before him for the dirt and blood blended them together. He watched as Chandra bravely pulled herself up onto her one good leg to greet the Commander.

"Colonel, great job! I wasn't sure if any of you would have made it."

"Sir, are we needed back in the fight?" asked Jones.

"Negative, Captain. The Russian forces are handling the centre. German and British armoured Corps are sweeping in from the north and Turkish and Yugoslavian units have entered at the south."

"My, God, then we've done it," Taylor whispered.

"You've done it, Major, you and all the fine men and women who held this river. Paris remains free. We have not won the war, but we have drawn a line in the sand."

"Where do we go from here, Sir?"

"For you, Captain, to a resting area east of the city. We are driving the enemy forces out but we can only continue so far. Paris has become the Bastion of Earth forces, it will be our base from henceforth. Vehicles are en route to carry the wounded. My thanks to you all, you have the respect and appreciation of the world. Major Taylor, please join me."

Mitch shrugged off the dust from his uniform, but it had little effect. He stepped through the rubble and to the vehicle as Phillips climbed aboard. He looked back to the troops one last time, giving them a nod and casual salute. They continued to watch the friendly forces surge west over the enemy's bridge to push the creatures out of the city.

* * *

Kelly sat at his desk just ten metres from Lewis. He tapped his fingers on his desk as he stared into space. He sat uneasily in his chair, still in full armour. They had been awaiting news of the great battle for France since it began. They knew that their survival was entirely dependent on the Earth troops' ability to halt the enemy's progress.

The room was utterly silent. They had gained a few small victories in ambushing Mechs with their new weapons, but were aware that they had made little progress. The Commander had his launcher in his lap, never letting it out of his sight. He said he kept it on him to show to all the colonists that he was fighting for their survival and freedom. It was only a half-truth. Kelly feared that the Mechs would breach their compound at any time.

"Sir, we're receiving a message!" shouted Lewis.

Kelly sprang into action, swivelling in his chair and leaping to his feet. He stopped and stared at the comms officer in anticipation. He dreaded the news just as much as he yearned for it.

"They've done it, Sir, Paris has held! They've driven the Mechs from the city!"

The room erupted in excitement, but Kelly just lowered he head as he fought back tears. He wondered if the onslaught would ever end. He knew that until the invaders had been stopped in a pitched battle that there was no hope. The comms officer looked at him.

"We've done it, Sir, we've beaten them!"

"I know, there is hope, and that is all we can ask."

* * *

Taylor stood at the window overlooking the recovery room where Parker was still connected to a host of machines. The Commander had arranged her transfer to a hospital north of Paris as the battle still raged. Phillips was aware that her survival and presence could do wonders for the unit, the Major in particular.

Passersby stared at his filthy clothes, his rifle was still slung over his shoulder. It was obvious that the officer had just endured a brutal fight. No one had the heart to tell him to clean himself up. Commander Phillips stood with him. He'd driven him there in his own vehicle.

"It is a delicate thing, Major, morale."

"Yes, Sir."

He didn't take his eyes of Eli.

"In the coming days, weeks, months or even years, we will need every soldier on God's Earth. You have done not just your country proud today, Major, but the entire world. I have arranged the best medical treatment for Sergeant Parker. The doctors here assure me that she will recover fully in time."

He turned and looked at the Commander confused. He'd hoped with all his heart for Eli to survive her wounds, but he had doubted her chances. He turned back to see her once again. Her eyes opened and she tilted her head just slightly to look at him through the glass. A smile lit up his face as he looked into her eyes.

At that moment he knew there was hope for them all.

Lightning Source UK Ltd.
Milton Keynes UK
UKOW022036160112

185480UK00003B/13/P